Book Two
in the
Sisters Redeemed Series

This Shadow

Jerusha Agen

This Shadow

© 2013 Jerusha Agen

ISBN-10:1938092546
ISBN-13:978-1-938092-54-1

All rights reserved. No part of this publication may be reproduced or transmitted in any form or by any means without written permission from the publisher.

This book is a work of fiction. Names, characters, places, and incidents are either products of the author's imagination or used fictitiously. Any similarity to actual people and/or events is purely coincidental.

Scripture quotations are from The Holy Bible, English Standard Version® (ESV®), copyright © 2001 by Crossway, a publishing ministry of Good News Publishers. Used by permission. All rights reserved.

Scriptures are taken from the Holy Bible, New International Version®, NIV®. Copyright © 1973, 1978, 1984 by Biblica, Inc.™ Used by permission of Zondervan. All rights reserved worldwide. www.zondervan.com

Published by Write Integrity Press, 130 Prominence Point Pkwy. #130-330, Canton, GA 30114.

www.WriteIntegrity.com

Printed in the United States of America.

Soli Deo Gloria

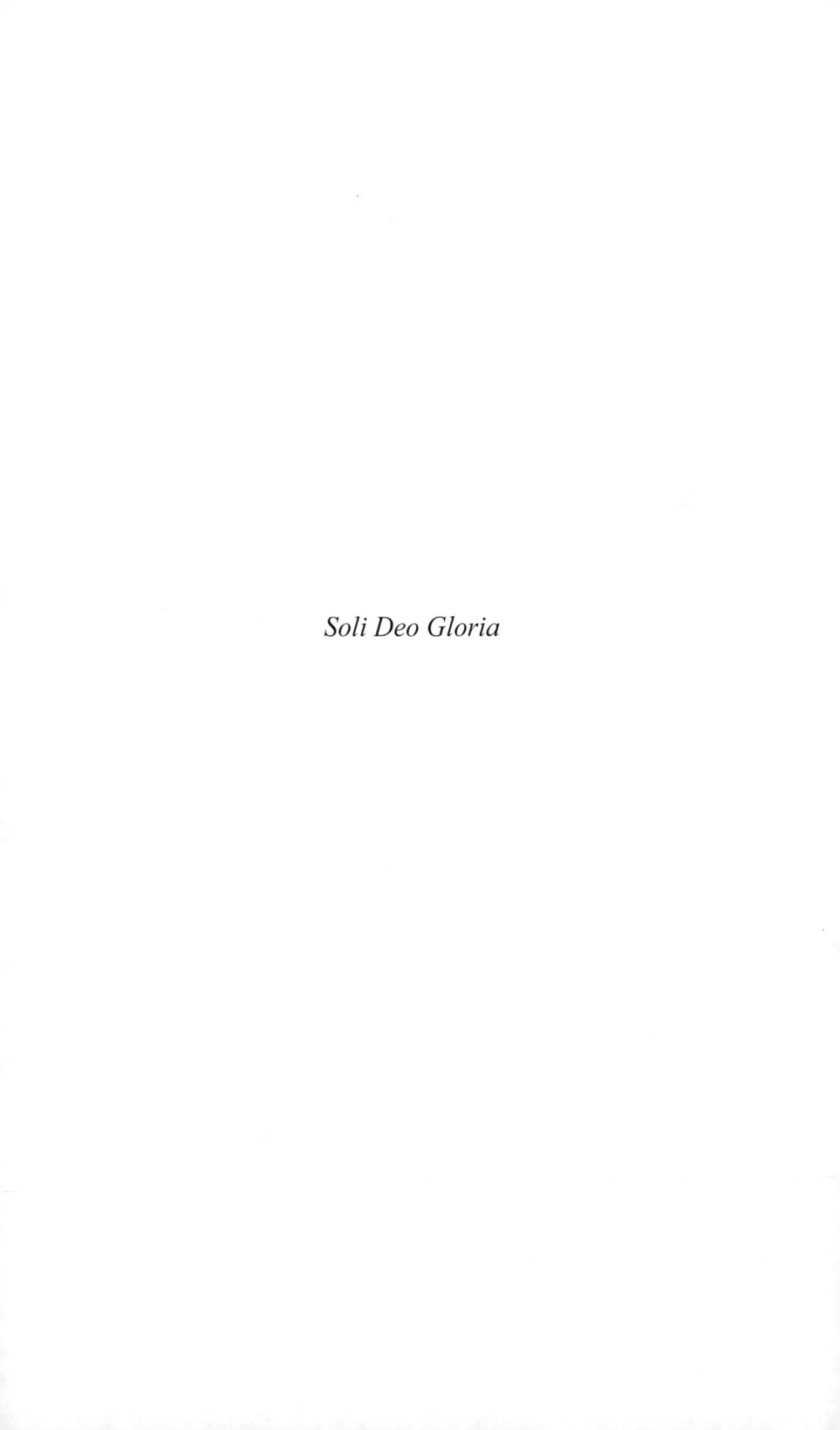

Acknowledgements

I would like to thank my friends and family for their support of my writing career, with all of its ups and downs. I especially have to thank my sisters and brothers in the Lord at New Hope Presbyterian Church: your enthusiasm and encouragement of my publication have been a blessing!

I want to extend a special thanks to two of my college professors, John Pennington and Laurie MacDiarmid: you each played an incalculable role in my development as a writer, and I thank you for your tireless effort in challenging me and your other students to excel. I wouldn't be where I am today without your guidance and instruction.

Thanks also to Carolyn Nothnagel for your help with making sure I got my teaching facts right. To all of my friends who are teachers and to all the educators in our schools, thank you for your dedication to positively shaping future generations.

To my mom: my endless thanks for your friendship and the godly example that you set. You are tirelessly willing to serve and support your family, giving us a palpable demonstration of unconditional love. God blessed me beyond measure when He gave me you for my mother.

Chapter One

*"Christ leads me through no darker rooms
than He went through before."*
– Richard Baxter ("Lord, It Belongs Not to My Care")

A girl's scream stopped Oriana Sanders mid-sentence.

"What was—" her sister, Nye, started to ask, but Oriana had already bolted for the door out of the dance studio.

Oriana ran across the small parking lot to the kids who clustered around something she couldn't see. She reached the outside of the ring the kids formed and looked over their heads.

Juan Castro and Dez Jennings stood in the middle, swinging at each other.

Oriana barely had time to register that they were fighting before Dez swung his leg and knocked the bigger boy off his feet.

In a split second, Dez was on the blacktop behind Juan, his arm wrapped tightly around the heavy boy's neck.

"Dez, stop!" Oriana pushed through the kids to reach the boys. She pulled on Dez's arm.

He stared down at Juan with a strange vacancy in his bloodshot eyes. His grip didn't loosen, though Juan kicked and squirmed.

"Dez, listen to me." Oriana tried to pull Juan from the hold just as a man's tanned hand appeared behind Dez and grabbed the boy by the back of his shirt, yanking him away.

Oriana's breath came back in a rush when normal color flooded Juan's cheeks.

He panted and put a hand to his throat.

"Are you okay?"

Juan nodded.

Oriana stood and looked to see who their rescuer was. "Nicanor?"

She had only seen Nicanor Pessoa once, at a distance, but his chiseled features and wavy black hair were not things a woman forgot. Now she found herself caught by his eyes—a stunning electric blue that had no business being among his dark, Argentine features.

His eyebrow arched slightly above one of those eyes, as if surprised she knew his name.

Heat rushed to her cheeks. She felt like she had just admitted to stalking him on Facebook, though she knew he wasn't actually on there since she had checked. She opened her mouth to say something, but his gaze dropped to the boy he held.

Dez grunted and squirmed in Nicanor's grip.

Oriana crouched in front of Dez, trying to push aside the questions that swirled in her mind about Nicanor's sudden appearance. She met the boy's glare straight-on. "I thought you meant it, Dez."

A startled lift of the eyebrows betrayed his tough-guy scowl.

She waited.

"What?" he finally muttered.

"You told me you weren't going to let your temper control you anymore. Remember?"

He looked down. "Nothing controls me." He jerked again, but the effort was hopeless.

"Then do you want to tell me why you were fighting with Juan?"

His jaw muscles clenched beneath his dark skin.

Stifling a sigh, she stood. "I want you to get in the van and stay there until we leave." She looked at Nicanor. "I think it's okay to let him go now."

Nicanor's eyebrow went up again, reminding her so much of Dez that she had to squelch a smile.

To reassure him, she spoke to Dez. "Can Mr. Pessoa let you go? Will you get in the van?"

Dez nodded, glaring at the blacktop.

Oriana gave Nicanor a small smile, and the stoic man slowly relaxed his grip.

Dez jerked away, flashing Nicanor a sneer before he turned and swaggered to the van as if he had just been named rapper of the year.

"He forgot his cap." LaTisha picked up the fallen cap from the blacktop and looked at Oriana with her big, long-lashed eyes. "Should I give it to him?"

"I'd rather you stay with me until we all go home. I'll hang on to it for him." Oriana took the cap LaTisha handed her and went back to where Juan still sat on the ground.

"Are you sure you're okay?"

"Yeah." He stood up as if he had forgotten he could, looking shaken but healthy.

"What was the fight about, Juan?"

His gaze dropped.

Oriana looked at the other kids, who immediately applied themselves to the job of avoiding her gaze. She knew better than to expect an answer, but she couldn't help hoping. She swallowed her disappointment and reminded herself to look on the bright side. Building trust with these kids was just going to take a little longer.

"Nicanor?"

Oriana turned to see her sister approach the silent rescuer. Nye didn't look nearly as surprised to see her old friend as Oriana had been. She was the picture of grace and confidence, as usual.

Oriana couldn't ignore the little twinge she felt when Nicanor's dark expression lightened slightly as he looked at Nye.

Honestly. Nye was very happily married, so Oriana

certainly had no reason to be jealous, if that's what her odd reaction meant.

"You came." Nye smiled at Nicanor. "Did you think about it?"

His head tilted in the smallest hint of a nod.

"You'll do it?" Nye's smile widened.

"Yes. For now."

Not trying to eavesdrop, Oriana couldn't help overhearing the oddly cryptic conversation.

"Wonderful. Thank you." Nye's voice was calm, but as she turned to walk to Oriana, the gleam in her eyes betrayed that she was considerably more excited than she was letting on.

"Everything okay?" Nye stopped by Oriana.

"I think so." Oriana tried to guess which topic Nye was referring to—the exotic heartthrob behind her or the unruly middle schoolers.

"Do you know what started it?"

Ah. The kids. Oriana made herself focus on her sister. "I have a pretty good idea." She lowered her voice. "They won't tell me, of course."

Nye looked at the children, who were regrouping into little cliques of two or three. "African-American versus Hispanic?"

Oriana smiled. Bless her sister's politically-correct heart. "Something like that." She spotted a glance from Nicanor and tried to catch his gaze. "Thanks for your help. I'm really glad you were here."

A small jerk of his chin was her only answer.

"I'll have to start advertising that Nye's Dance Studio has its own bouncer." Nye turned her twinkling gaze on Oriana as she laughed.

Hearing her sister laugh and joke after so many years watching her grieve the loss of her fiancé was enough to distract Oriana from Nicanor's lack of response. She was looking at a miracle in Nye's smile, and she wasn't going to let being ignored by a gorgeous tango dancer spoil the moment.

Nye caught Oriana's look. "I know. It's good to see me smile again."

"I don't think I'll ever get used to it."

"Our God is great."

Oriana's heart swelled at the statement from her sister who was once so bitter at God. "You can say that again." Oriana's gaze fell on Nicanor behind Nye as he turned and headed toward the studio.

"Sorry."

Oriana looked at her sister, realizing too late that she had been caught watching.

"I should have introduced you. I felt bad I didn't get to at the wedding."

"He does seem to skedaddle whenever I'm around."

"It's not you."

"Not like it matters at all, of course." Oriana waved her hand dismissively. "I've scared off cuter guys than him," she lied.

"Miss Sanders? Are we going now?"

Nye squished her lips together, only partially holding back a laughing smile as Oriana turned to see eleven-year-old Maria at her side.

Had the little girl heard that? Tossing Nye a mortified look, Oriana tried to pretend nothing was amiss. "Yes, sweetie, we're going now. Okay, kids," she called to the others, "everyone in the van!"

Oriana glanced at Nye. "Are we still welcome here in the future?"

Nye swept back a renegade strand of blonde hair from her bun and tucked it behind her ear. "You know the answer to that. With me at least." She tossed a pointed gaze at the studio where Nicanor had gone, her eyes twinkling.

Oriana wrinkled her nose at her sister. "Thanks." She glanced at the thin sweater Nye wore. "Now get inside before you freeze to death."

She followed the group of kids as they trudged to the van, glad she already had her jacket on when the commotion started. Fall was quickly turning into winter.

She tried to resist a last look over her shoulder at the studio. If only she could stay and find out what Nicanor was doing here. Seemed strange he would just suddenly show up like that. And she had no idea what the cryptic little conversation between him and her sister meant. She'd have to call Nye as soon as she got home tonight.

Putting such thoughts on hold, she focused on counting her kids and planning what she would say to them about their behavior.

Something touched her hand. Startled, she looked down to see Maria gently grasp her hand with small fingers. Joy surged through Oriana and put energy in her step as she closed her hand around the little girl's. Praise the Lord that just when things started to look dark, He always sent a burst of light.

───❦───

Nicanor heard Nye enter the dance studio, but he couldn't pull his eyes away from the window, watching as Oriana disappeared into the van.

"She'll be fine." Nye quietly stopped beside him.

He turned away from the glass. Nye's blonde dancer beauty was such a startling contrast to her sister. It seemed strange that Oriana was a brunette. When Nye used to speak of her younger sibling years before, he had always pictured a sweet little imp with blonde flowing hair like the older sister who spoke so lovingly of her. That image had not prepared him for the moment at Nye's wedding two months ago when he saw the real Oriana—a vibrant woman with thick waves of brown hair and so much spirit in her dark eyes that he couldn't look at them for long. If her name hadn't been listed in the wedding program, he would never have guessed the woman standing up as Nye's maid of honor was her little sister. She was as pretty as Nye but had an open, lively face and an obvious passion for life—a crackling energy that was nothing like Nye's quiet elegance and private, controlled ways.

"She knows how to handle those kids." Nye watched him.

"She teaches them?"

Nye nodded. "She's a Language Arts teacher at Lincoln Middle School, and she's in charge of the afterschool program for at-risk sixth graders. It's in the roughest part of Harper, which is worse than you might think for a city this size. She started bringing the kids here for lessons three weeks ago."

"Do they often fight?"

"Oh, no." Nye's eyes widened. "This was the first time anything like that happened. Well, they squabble a little, but I hadn't seen anything physical before. I'm glad you showed up when you did."

Lucky that he had. No one as naively cheerful as Oriana appeared to be could handle a group of street kids. "Of course." Oriana was in over her pretty head. He saw that black kid's bloodshot eyes. Oriana had no idea what her students were into.

"Maybe you should help her then."

Nicanor jerked to meet her blue-eyed gaze.

She smiled. "You think she's in over her head, so why don't you help her?"

He stared at her. Nye had always been perceptive, but he

didn't think of her as a mind reader.

She laughed. "Have you forgotten how much time we've spent together? Dante isn't the only one who learned how to interpret your silences, you know."

His gut twisted at Dante's name. She could use it so easily now. Even smiling as she said it. Smiling at him. He whipped away and headed for the open doorway that he could see led to the dance floor.

"Wait a minute."

"I'll help you get ready for your class."

"My next class isn't for twenty minutes yet. And you haven't even been here ten. You don't have to start working right away." Nye caught up with him as he entered the room and began to pick up the dance shoes the children must have used.

She stopped in the doorway and watched him. "It will be wonderful having you here. I can really use another instructor."

"The studio is doing well, then."

"Yes, God's really blessing it."

Nicanor hoped so. Nye deserved to be blessed.

"What do you want me to tell Terry if he calls?"

Nicanor rubbed at a mark on one of the small shoes with his thumb. "He isn't my agent anymore."

"Oh." Nye's tone was cautious, but Nicanor knew she wouldn't press. "I'm sorry to hear that."

He picked up another pair of shoes and looked at her.

"Show me where these go?"

She smiled. "Sure. Then we'll look at the schedule and see which classes you'd like to teach."

She was so different. The Nye he knew in New York was not the same woman who stood before him now. He didn't understand the change. Perhaps finding someone else. Her new husband must make her happy. He wondered if this new love was enough to make up for what had happened, for what he had done.

Nicanor paused at the doorway when he reached Nye, and she looked at him for a moment.

Then she smiled again, that new happy smile. "Thanks for coming, Nicanor."

If only he could tell her. Her smile just made his pain worse, twisting like a knife in his open wound when she didn't know the extent of his guilt. When she didn't know that she should hate him. At least for the moment, she could keep smiling.

Jerusha Agen

Chapter Two

"Again, Jesus spoke to them, saying, 'I am the light of the world. Whoever follows me will never walk in darkness, but will have the light of life.'"
– John 8:12

Oriana stared at Principal Harry Stewart as he lifted his hands and leaned slightly back in the chair behind the towers of paper on his desk.

"I'm not happy about this, but I really have no other choice." His tone lacked enough remorse to be convincing.

"We both know that's not true." Oriana scooted forward on the chair facing his desk and met his gaze. "Yes, the kids had a little scuffle, but that could've happened here just as well as away from the school. You know that."

"Yes, but I also know the rules. I should put Dez Jennings on suspension, too, but I'll let it go one more time for your sake. According to regulations, an incident like this requires that I suspend all class activities off school grounds."

Oriana crossed her arms. "You mean the regulations for *my* class."

He shifted and wiped his index finger under his nose. "Not necessarily."

She stared past his glasses at his eyes.

He met her challenging stare, a hint of doubt in his gaze.

The corner of her mouth tugged into a smile, ruining her short-lived attempt at a stern expression. "Okay, Harry. You win."

His shoulders relaxed as he let out a breath.

"Afraid I was going to let you have it, weren't you?"

He shook his head with a smile. "Not you, Oriana."

"Uh-huh." Oriana popped up and headed for the closed door. "Let me know when we can get out of the attic that you banished us to."

"I've been meaning to find you a better classroom. I'll—"

"…work on it," she finished for him as she opened the door. "I know, Harry."

"Oh, and Oriana …"

She turned back to see him holding up a finger.

"This doesn't look too good for your new program." He raised a second finger. "Two strikes so far. You know what happens on three."

She nodded. "Have a nice day, Harry." She closed the door behind her, mustering a small smile for Gladys, who watched from behind her desk as Oriana exited the waiting area for Harry's office.

Oriana went down the hall to her Language Arts classroom, a luxury suite compared to the one for her afterschool kids, but her mind was not on the grammar lesson she had prepared. She replayed the conversation with Harry in her head. She was no coward, but arguing further would have been futile. She knew the regulations as well as Harry, and he was right. He had already given her a grace period after the last public incident—another Dez blowup.

She grabbed her hair and pulled it away from her face and neck, then let the thick waves drop again as she reached the classroom.

"Hi, Miss Sanders." Ginny, a twelve-going-on-sixteen-year-old, smiled as she passed Oriana to enter the room.

"Hi, Ginny." Oriana took a deep breath and tried to concentrate on the task at hand. But as she stepped into the classroom, the discouragement and frustration that had driven her to focus on the afterschool program washed over her once again. In her three Language Arts and two Social Studies classes every long day, she had a mix of students like the one before her. The kids were so young, but they were already trying hard to live up to their labels—the jock, the clown, the geek, teacher's pet, bully, gangbanger.

Oriana looked away from the noisy group and went to the blackboard at the front of the class. She started writing out the day's lesson, biting her lip as she held back the tears that pricked at her eyes. Education was important, but she wasn't teaching any of these hurting kids what they really needed to know—how to live a better way than what they learned on the streets.

She turned to face the class and quiet them down. Even though her passion was with the afterschool program and the possibilities it offered, she owed it to these students to be as present and enthusiastic as she could.

By the end of fifth period, Oriana was thankful for the undying pep that had prompted her dad to dub her "The Energizer Bunny" when she was young. Trying to get these cynical, street-wise kids interested in literature, grammar, or writing was like expecting a Marmaduke comic strip to morph into *War and Peace*. At least that's what it felt like on a day like this.

Trying to let go of the conflicts she had already encountered with her so-called "better" students, she gathered up her books to head for the hardest, but most rewarding, challenge of her day.

She entered the hall and shifted her tote bag out of the way as a student brushed past. Moving against the traffic of kids fleeing the school, Oriana started up the hall toward the stairs.

"Hi, Miss Sanders." Trista, another excelling student, stood with her other teacher Sandra in the doorway of a classroom and waved.

Sandra smiled as Oriana passed by. "Still on for lunch tomorrow?"

"Planning on it at noon." Oriana returned their smiles as she avoided looking past the open doorway at the large, clean classroom behind them—the reminder of what her kids should be able to have. She wasn't even allowed to use her Language Arts room for the afterschool class. As if the students had some sort of plague.

She sighed. Teaching wasn't about the room. It was about helping the kids. Kids like Dez. The reminder of the group that was supposed to be gathering in their makeshift classroom at that moment was enough to make her pick up her pace. To leave that bunch alone was never a good idea.

"Hey, Oriana."

"Hi." She nodded to Davis Wentworth who stood near the stairs talking to Harrison, one of his favorite eighth-grade basketball players.

"How's your pretend class going?" His mocking grin told her the question wasn't worth answering.

As if PE was more of a real class than the afterschool program. "Cute, Davis." She gave him the most tolerant smile she could manage and didn't stop to chat.

"I hear you've added dancing now," he called. "That should soften 'em up."

She rolled her eyes at his cackle and refused to look back as she started the trek up three flights of stairs. Davis was the most vocal, but sadly not the only teacher in the opposition. It had taken the first two years Oriana had been at Lincoln to get her proposal for an afterschool enrichment program approved, and getting the go-ahead still didn't mean that everyone supported it.

Many of the teachers thought she was wasting her time, and others thought she was babying the kids or even rewarding them for the bad behavior that landed them in detention. What an awful word—"detention." Her goal was to flip it on its head, so these kids would learn to see school as a positive place to be and learn that mistakes were opportunities to change.

It would be no easy task to extract that lesson when she broke the news to the kids about their dance classes. Oriana had been more excited than her students when she first told them they were going to take dance lessons. The idea wasn't her own—dance had been taught to at-risk students for years now—but the program was a successful one that Oriana was thrilled to implement with such a young group of kids. She hoped it would teach them how to relate to each other better, to treat people with respect, to be disciplined and work together.

In the three weeks they had been going to Nye's studio, Oriana could tell the impressionable eleven and twelve-year-olds were starting to like the classes a lot. The sessions were a change of pace from being confined in their dark and drafty room on the school's third floor for their afterschool hours. And the art of dance was a far cry from anything they found on the streets or at home.

"Hey, Miss Sanders."

Oriana looked up from the steps in front of her.

LaTisha stood on the landing before the third set of stairs, her thumbs hooked through her backpack straps as she watched

Oriana with those big eyes.

Oriana smiled. "You're punctual as always."

LaTisha responded with a proud grin.

A small pang tweaked Oriana's chest at the sight of LaTisha's hairstyle. She had managed to pull it into a bun like Nye's, no small effort with LaTisha's African-American hair type. Several of the girls had started the same, sweet imitation recently. Nye was a magnet for the young preteens, just as Oriana was sure she would be.

"Are the other kids in the classroom?" Oriana reached the landing and paused by her student.

"Don't know. I didn't get that far."

"Okay." Oriana nodded and squelched another smile. Like so many of the kids in Oriana's class, LaTisha was in that awkward phase of still being a child, but wanting to behave and be treated like she was a woman. A holdover from the little girl part was apparently still being afraid of the dark.

Oriana led the way up the last flight of stairs and pretended not to notice when LaTisha shrunk behind her as they reached the top. Oriana could see why LaTisha was frightened. The hallway that greeted them when they turned the corner at the top of the stairs was dark and shadowed, thanks to no windows and only a small bulb that flickered a distance away, outside the classroom. Rusted lockers, some of them with dented doors hanging from the hinges lined the walls, interrupted by a few dark rooms that were locked, used only for storage.

Oriana hated the message that the location of their afterschool room sent these kids. She hoped they were too young to realize what it meant to be sentenced to the floor that the school had chosen not to renovate. These kids were worth effort and attention. All they needed was some light in their lives.

Oriana stopped, causing LaTisha to bump into her from behind. "LaTisha, look," Oriana said in stage whisper.

LaTisha slowly peeked around Oriana, her eyes even larger than normal. "What?" she whispered back.

"See that light?"

"Uh-huh."

"Do you know what it reminds me of?"

LaTisha looked up at Oriana, then at the bulb. "A scary movie?"

"No. It reminds me of people," Oriana said in a normal voice.

LaTisha stood up straighter and moved to Oriana's side, confusion and curiosity getting the better of her fear. "What?"

Oriana walked toward the dim bulb, this time with LaTisha next to her. "Some people look awfully dark and even scary from the outside, but you know what they need?"

They stopped under the light, and LaTisha stared up at it. She shrugged.

"They need a new light. A stronger one that will brighten

their lives and last forever."

"How do they get that?"

"Do you remember when you went to my church? And we talked about Jesus in Sunday school?"

"I thought you weren't supposed to talk about Jesus with us." Dez appeared in the doorway of their classroom and leaned against the doorframe, a black bandana sticking out from under his red baseball cap.

An acrid stench, different from the usual musty smell Oriana could not get rid of, wafted out of the room behind him. "And you aren't supposed to smoke cigarettes." Oriana stepped past him and looked around. The former library, from back in the day when the school actually had enough attendance to have use for such a thing, appeared to be as she had left it. The two round tables still had the scraps of wood wedged under their legs to keep them from wobbling, and the mismatched, rusted folding chairs were mostly in place.

Three stray chairs near the window drew her attention to the daylight coming through. The window was so filthy on the outside that she could never count on it to allow much light in the room, except when the weather was warm enough to have the window open.

The air was freezing today, but the window was open a crack anyway. "Okay." Oriana's voice was firm as she scanned the rest of the room. "Antonio and Brayden, you can come out now."

The two boys slowly materialized, reluctantly crawling out from behind a row of empty shelves that stood perpendicular to the wall. At least the boys had the sense to look guilty.

"Really, guys? Smoking leaves a smell on your clothes, too, so the window doesn't help. Antonio, close it, and Brayden, put the chairs back." Oriana turned to Dez, who had pulled out a chair by the table and slumped in it, his arms crossed over his chest. "I'm disappointed, guys." She looked mostly at Dez as she spoke. "You are all too smart to smoke cigarettes."

"What about pot?" Dez asked with a sarcastic sneer as the other boys snickered.

LaTisha shot Dez an alarmed glance before she spotted Oriana watching and dropped her gaze to the floor.

Oriana went to the table and sat down opposite Dez. She met his gaze. "You are definitely too smart to do that, Dez." Her heart sank at the redness of his eyes. She hoped she had been imagining things yesterday at Nye's studio. *Dear Lord, he's only twelve ...*

Dez looked away, probably realizing what she might see.

She'd like to think his reaction signaled a bout of conscience. He wasn't lost yet, even if he had started on marijuana.

She stood. "Dez, I'd like to talk to you in the hall for a moment, please." She walked to the door and turned back.

"Antonio, you're in charge 'til I get back. It'll be just a minute." She looked at Dez, who still hadn't moved. "Dez."

He rolled his eyes and slowly stood, swaggering to the hall.

She moved a few feet away from the door down the hallway, hoping that was far enough for the other students not to be able to eavesdrop. "We need to talk about what happened at the dance studio."

Jaw tensed, he kept his head turned to the side.

"That was a gang thing, wasn't it?"

"I ain't—I'm not in a gang."

Oriana's hope increased at his grammatical self-correction—a sign he still cared a little what she thought. She didn't want to believe he could have hardened and changed so fast. "But your brother is, right?"

He shrugged.

"And Juan's is, too."

He worked hard to avoid her gaze while she tried to meet his.

"Dez, would you look at me, please?" She waited while he stared at the floor.

Slowly, painfully, he lifted his gaze to her face.

"I remember a boy who used to smile and laugh. He was honest with me and smart enough to get good grades. He brought LaTisha to Sunday school at church a few times and stuck up for me with the other students in class. I think he was pretty happy." She paused to let it sink in. "That was you, Dez."

He swallowed.

"Do you remember being that person?"

His gaze shifted away again and dropped to the floor.

"Things are only going to get worse if you keep going down this road. Gangs just mean violence and drugs and hate. They'll kill you, Dez." She didn't want to say such things to a twelve-year-old, but she had to get through. "Don't you want something better?"

"James is happy." Dez's tone held a defensive edge.

"Are you sure he is?"

He shrugged again. "Yeah."

"Well, there are different kinds of happiness. Some are more real than others."

He looked up at her, a mixture of challenge and question in his bloodshot eyes. "What kind do you have?"

"The kind that comes from Jesus. It never ends." She knew she could get in trouble for talking about her faith, but she wasn't in the classroom right now, and she had never been one to let regulations silence her from offering the help these kids really needed.

"James says people like you talk about Jesus 'cause you never had anything bad happen to you."

That wasn't a surprise, coming from Dez's gangbanger brother. "I talk about Jesus because he died to save me.

Because He loves me. If Jesus is in your heart, you can have joy no matter what anyone does to you."

"James says you gotta make 'em pay."

"Then you'll only be hurting yourself more."

He crossed his arms, his eyebrows drawing together. "That doesn't make sense."

A rustling sound came from behind Oriana.

Maria stood a couple feet away and wiped at her nose, her oversized winter jacket making another crumpling noise as she moved.

"Hi, Maria." Oriana turned toward her.

Maria sniffed and smiled shyly. "Hi, Miss Sanders."

Oriana looked at Dez. "We can talk more later." She smiled at Maria. "Let's go to class."

Oriana thought she might melt at the way the petite girl slipped her hand in Oriana's and pressed close to her side as they walked into the classroom.

Maria was too shy to risk more than quick glances at the other kids as they entered.

Oriana had to stop herself from putting an arm around Maria's shoulders in a hug—that kind of physical contact wasn't allowed between teachers and students these days. Showing favoritism wouldn't help either of them, anyway. She wished she could do something to ease the situation for Maria, but she was also relieved that the sweet girl wasn't pals with the tougher kids in her class.

Maria's innocence and kindness could do some good for LaTisha, if LaTisha wasn't so set against being friendly with Maria. LaTisha's whole demeanor changed as soon as the other girl arrived. She rested a hand on her hip like a grown women as she stared at Maria with challenge in her eyes.

Oriana guided Maria to a chair by the far table and watched as her four other students meandered into the room, some shrinking as they entered and others swaggering with chips the size of redwood logs on their shoulders.

Juan carried one as big as a sequoia tree when he walked in, eyes locking with Dez's glare as he went to the table on the far side of the room—the table where the Hispanic kids naturally grouped unless Oriana split them up.

Oriana put on a smile to greet the newcomers, hoping it covered her sadness. Every day was a battle for these kids. How was she going to dish out another blow with the news about the dance lessons? It would be one more reason for them to forget about school, education, reaching for something better. One more time of someone telling them they weren't good enough. She just couldn't do it.

When Jonique Farris came in sporting another imitation of Nye's hairstyle, the light bulb turned on in Oriana's mind. The dance classes wouldn't have to end at all if Oriana could talk her sister into coming to the school. It would mean a hassle for Nye, though, and might not work with her class schedules. At least Oriana wouldn't have to break any bad news to her kids today—not until she knew for sure if Nye could do it. No bad news except for some punishment she would have to come up with for Dez and the other two smoking boys. But what was there left to do when they were already in detention?

With that familiar challenge as her next project, Oriana flashed her brightest smile to the class. "Okay, everyone, find a chair, and we'll get started."

Oriana still hadn't come up with a suitable disciplinary action by the time she walked through the crisp air to her car on the street, carrying a tote with books and her purse slung over the other shoulder. Dez had already received more discipline from school than most kids, and it didn't seem to have done an ounce of good. She could try to meet with his mother again, but Oriana hadn't been able to get the woman to come in when she had attempted that before.

She had to do something. She had watched Dez go from being a sweet kid to a gangster apprentice, despite her efforts to give him the love, attention, and firm rules he needed. He was even already in mandatory counseling sessions. If he had started using, Oriana had to try something different. He wouldn't talk to her anymore, let alone listen—

The ring of the cellphone cut through her thoughts just as she reached her car parked next to the sidewalk. Of course. She set the tote on the hood and fumbled in her purse for the phone, which slipped out of her mitten-clad hand when she grabbed it. With a frustrated grunt, she took off her wool mitten and grasped the elusive gizmo.

"Hey, lady. Looking for something?"

Oriana looked up to see two young men watching her from the sidewalk, their grins and the sleazy glint in their eyes telling her they were not offering help. Bangers from the look of them. She quickly put the phone to her ear and answered.

"Took you long enough." Nye's teasing voice was a welcome sound.

"Yeah. Mittens and cell phones don't mix." She glanced at the men, careful not to stare as they watched her and made comments to each other that were apparently very funny. "Can you hang on a sec?"

"Sure."

Oriana grabbed the car keys from her pocket and unlocked the door.

The two guys moved closer to Oriana's car as she reached for the tote. She couldn't tell if they were just going to cross the street or approach her. Looking like she was trying to get away might be asking for it, so she kept her breathing even and her movements casual.

As they neared the back end of her car, the taller one looked right at Oriana and made a disgusting comment that she supposed was meant to be some kind of come-on.

This Shadow

"No, thanks." She tossed the tote across to the passenger seat, not caring if the books dumped out. "Got a phone call." She waved her cell phone and put it to her ear as she slipped into the car and shut the door.

Locking it immediately, she breathed again when the bangers swaggered across the street. "Thanks for waiting," she said into the phone, as she watched one of the men grin at her over his shoulder.

"Did some guy just say what I think he did?"

"Sadly, yes." Just noticing her frigid fingers, she switched the phone to her left hand and started the car.

"Who was he?"

"I don't know. Some guy outside the school."

"No wonder Mom worries about you teaching there."

"Yes, but *you* always understand," Oriana hinted, as she switched the phone back to her right side, grateful that her older sister wasn't the mothering type.

"Sure." There was a knowing amusement in Nye's tone. "Well, speaking of men ..."

Oriana sucked in an excited breath. "Nicanor." All thoughts of the bangers were instantly replaced by the mystery of her heartthrob rescuer. "Yes, I've been dying to know. Why didn't you answer your phone last night? What's he doing here? Did you know he was coming? Why didn't you warn me?"

"Hold on." Nye laughed. "One question at a time, please. I

didn't answer because my phone's battery was dead—"

"Again," Oriana inserted.

"Yes, again. And no, I did not know he was coming, which is why I didn't warn you."

"Oh. So he just showed up unannounced?"

"Yes."

Oriana narrowed her eyes. "You didn't seem surprised."

"I was ... a little. But that's just the way Nicanor is."

"So you did know he might come."

"I thought it was a possibility, but I wasn't holding out hope."

"A possibility?" Oriana tapped the steering wheel with her mitten-covered finger. "There's something you're not telling me."

"Well, at the wedding, I asked if he would stay and be an instructor at the studio."

"You did? Why didn't you tell me?"

"He didn't say he'd do it. Just that he'd think about it. That could mean anything with Nicanor. Then he went back to New York right away, so I thought that might be the end of it. I didn't want to get your hopes up."

Oriana stopped tapping the wheel. Oops. So much for not exposing her silly crush to her sister. She tried to cover the best she could. "Why would it get my hopes up? I don't even know the man."

Nye paused. "True." She managed to say the word without

a hint of suspicion.

Thank the Lord that Oriana's sister was much more sensitive than she was. If their roles were reversed, Oriana would have pushed a lot harder or at least pointed to the obvious signs that she liked Nicanor. Tact was always more Nye's thing.

"Sooo, now he's here to stay?" Oriana tried to keep her voice level to avoid indicating any undue interest.

"That's never really a sure thing with Nicanor, but it sounds like he's here for at least a little while."

Oriana turned down the heater fan, tired of the cold air numbing her denim-clad legs. She wished she could start driving to get the heater warmed up, but she didn't want to risk another accident. Not that talking on the phone while driving was even the cause of her crash the winter before, but she had learned the importance of alert driving, especially when there was snow involved.

"Oriana …"

Oriana wasn't sure she liked the hesitant note in her sister's usually confident tone.

"I feel like I should warn you … about Nicanor."

"Warn me?"

"He can be a very nice person, but he's also a little rough. Dante was much closer to him than I was, but I know he was always troubled, always had some darkness hanging over him."

"Nye, troubled and rough is what I deal with every day."

Oriana looked out the windshield at the graffiti painted on the dirty brick walls of the school.

"Yes, I know. I'm just saying that he was into some bad things. His lifestyle was never very ... clean."

"He isn't a Christian, right?" Oriana's question was matter-of-fact.

"No."

"Then I wouldn't get involved. Nothing more than friendship. You know that." Oriana needed the reminder as much as her sister.

Nye breathed a sigh of relief. "Oh, good. I'm glad you're more solid than I was."

"Just be glad you always picked Christian guys when you fell in love."

Nye laughed. "Thank the Lord for that. Actually," her tone turned serious, "if you want to pray for Nicanor, I'd really appreciate it."

"You're worried about him?"

"Yes, I am. He was struggling before Dante died, and then after cutting him off for three years the way I did, I don't know what he went through ... He just seems more lost than I've ever seen him."

"Of course I'll pray for him."

"Thanks."

"And I could use prayer, too." Oriana shivered.

"Oh?"

"Yeah, pray that I don't freeze in my car before I can start driving."

Nye laughed for what felt like a minute. "I'll let you go, then," Nye said between chuckles, "but I was going to ask you over for dinner tonight."

"Sure you were. You just want to keep talking. Doesn't that husband of yours ever talk to you?"

"Once in a while," Nye joked in return. "Just be here at six."

"Yes, ma'am."

"Mom and Dad are coming and bringing Russell, too."

Oriana smiled at the prospect of getting to see the man she considered her grandfather-in-law. "Really? What's the occasion?"

"You'll find out when you get here."

"Ooh, I love a good mystery," Oriana said with exaggerated excitement.

"Funny. See you at six."

Oriana's smile dropped as soon as she hung up. She had forgotten to tell Nye about the dance classes getting cancelled. Another topic for dinner, then.

As she looked over her shoulder and pulled her car out onto the street, she wondered what the dinner was all about. Nye hadn't responded as Oriana thought she would if the invitation was simply for a casual meal. Oriana's mind raced over the possibilities. She wasn't good at waiting.

Jerusha Agen

Chapter Three

> *"If I hope for Sheol as my house,*
> *if I make my bed in darkness,*
> *if I say to the pit, 'You are my father,'*
> *and to the worm, 'My mother,' or 'My sister,'*
> *where then is my hope?"*
> – Job 17:13-15a

Nicanor stared at the clock. The numbers slowly changed, painfully dragging toward ten o'clock, the earliest he could take his sleeping pill without having it wear off before morning. Still two hours to go.

He got up from the mattress on the floor and went three steps to the window of the one-room apartment. The street below was nearly as dark as the windows in the apartment building across from it. Snow had turned to black slush that was pushed up along the sidewalks where clusters of gang bangers passed periodically, creating enough noise with their jeers and cussing to make their presence known to the neighborhood.

The city that Nicanor had seen when he came for Nye's wedding and stayed at a hotel was very different from the decayed depression outside his window. Even a wholesome place like Harper had its guilty secrets.

His cell phone rang where it sat on the chipped counter of the kitchen area. He didn't have to look to see who the caller was. Nicanor was not up to a lecture from Terry or another attempt to talk him out of his "destructive spiral," as the agent called it. Terry had said he was done with Nicanor several times in the past few months, but he kept coming back, always demanding. "You owe me" was Terry's favorite phrase.

The ringing finally stopped as Nicanor made a mental note to switch the phone's settings to vibrate. He turned away from the window and scanned the dingy walls of his small living space. At least the apartment was bigger than the little closet he could barely afford in New York. With his thin mattress already rolled out on the floor and a blanket on top, it reminded him of his first U.S. apartment, the one he had shared with Dante as roommates. Even splitting the rent didn't leave enough for the two young, unknown tango dancers to buy real beds.

The memory twisted in Nicanor's gut and brought the sting of moisture to his eyes. If only he could go back. If he could undo what he had done. He'd give anything. Everything.

The walls closed in around him. He had to get out. Maybe a smoke. He would need more cigarettes first. He only had a few crumpled bills in his jeans pocket, but his credit card should still work. It would be enough to get what he needed.

This Shadow

He picked up his jacket from the floor next to the mattress and left the apartment, not bothering to lock it. He pushed through the putrid-smelling hallway, his head down, avoiding eye contact with the few people he passed who appeared just as eager to avoid him. Maybe this neighborhood was a good fit for him after all. He certainly didn't deserve any better.

The cold air felt good against his hot cheeks when he walked out the door onto the sidewalk. He fished in the pocket of the light leather jacket he carried and found one cigarette left. He lit it as he walked in the direction of where he thought he had seen a small liquor store.

A group of four Latinos came down the sidewalk toward him, sizing him up. The small-time punks were like a child's dress up version of the toughs he had seen in his lifetime, but he supposed they could still be a problem. He didn't look at them as they passed, and they didn't bother him.

That was the approach that got him through the store without incident, past the gruff old man behind the counter who watched Nicanor with beady yellow eyes above a red-tipped nose. The same approach got him through most of his life in Argentina and New York. Life was the same everywhere. It never changed. At least not for him.

He stopped outside the store and set the paper bag of purchases on the ground beside him. Probably not a smart move if he wanted to keep them, but he wasn't so desperate as to think that a bottle of cheap whiskey and two packs of cigarettes were valuables. He put another cigarette between his lips and lit it. He took a long drag, trying to ignore the memories that swirled in his head.

Dancers shouldn't smoke, Dante said so many times.

Nicanor watched the smoke drift in front of him but saw only the image of Dante's grin, an attempt to hide the concern in his eyes. Nicanor couldn't even smoke without Dante being there, haunting him.

He threw the cigarette on the ground and crushed it under his foot.

Two bangers met farther down the sidewalk, standing close and glancing around. They briefly shook hands, obviously exchanging something. Nicanor didn't need to be a genius to know what that something was. He picked up the bag to start the walk back to the apartment before he could get tempted. Maybe living in this neighborhood was not such a good idea after all.

But Nye had looked happy to see him. Strange to see someone brighten like that at the sight of him. He hadn't known what kind of welcome, if any, to expect. She had seemed so peaceful at the wedding, even said that she was wrong to blame him. He didn't see how she could mean that, but if she did, it was only because she didn't know the truth.

The street was getting quieter, without even a street thug to distract him from the endless torment of his thoughts. Why did he even bother? Why go on like this? No one would care if he were dead.

He reached the apartment building and let himself in. Odors better left unidentified assaulted him as he went up the littered stairway. Trying to think only of putting one foot in front of the other, he climbed to the second floor.

No one would care. His agony would end.

He shut the apartment door behind him and set the bag on the floor.

No. Ending it would be too easy. He wouldn't have paid for what he had done. It would be the coward's way out. His father always said he was a coward.

He pulled the bottle out of the bag and opened it. He pressed it to his lips, forcing himself to swallow the liquid. How did his father drink so much whiskey? Nicanor could never get used to it, but it did dull the pain. He set the bottle on the floor and went to the bathroom.

Standing at the sink, he filled the paper cup he had found when he moved in and tried to rinse out the whiskey taste. The acrid city water didn't taste much better. He looked up with a grimace as he swallowed and spotted his reflection.

Why did the only furniture in the apartment have to be a mirror? The face staring back at him looked as it should—haggard, worn, and guilty.

You killed her. The words his father had spit at him so many times echoed in his mind. *God should have taken you instead. It is your fault she is dead.*

The words pierced Nicanor's soul as he stared at himself.

He launched his fist into the glass. The mirror shattered around his hand, falling in hundreds of pieces into the sink and on the floor. The sting of his cut fingers brought a small relief, a distraction from the agony in his heart. He looked down, past his bleeding hand to the glass on the floor. One shard was still large enough for him to catch a bit of his reflection.

His father got one thing right. It was the face of a murderer.

Chapter Four

> "Light dawns in the darkness for the upright;
> he is gracious, merciful, and righteous."
> – Psalm 112:4

"You're pregnant?" Oriana squealed and dashed around the table to hug Nye where she sat.

"Well, congratulations!" Their father bounced up from his chair and shook Cullen's hand.

Nye's husband grinned from ear to ear and cheerfully allowed his father-in-law to handle his arm like a water pump. Cullen's grandfather, Russell, put his hand on his grandson's shoulder from where he sat beside him, his lips scrunching to hold back emotion.

Oriana's mom wasn't so successful. She sat at the end of the table with tears running down her face.

"Mom," Oriana smiled, "this is *good* news."

She shook her head. "I know. I'm just so happy!"

Nye got up and went around the table to hug her mother. "Thanks, Mom."

Oriana's eyes started to moisten, too, as she watched them. There was a time when she never thought she would see her sister and mother do anything but argue. Thank the Lord for miracles. And for Cullen's part in helping Nye get over the loss of Dante.

Oriana went over to her brother-in-law and gave him a hug. "Congrats, bro." She gave him a cheeky grin as she pulled back.

He smiled back. "Thanks, sis."

Her heart warmed at his teasing response. She always knew it would be fun to have a brother. "Pretty fast work." She winked.

"Oriana!" Nye chided, her face warming.

"Well, it is." Oriana grinned, not the least bit sorry.

"Before you say anything else shocking, why don't you help me get the dessert?" Nye sent her sister a good-humored stare of censorship, her cheeks still prettily pink.

"Yes, ma'am." Oriana obediently trailed Nye to the kitchen, smiling at the sound of Jordan's tags jingling as the large German shepherd followed them.

Walking into the kitchen was like coming home. The ivory-colored cabinets, even the swirled pattern of the vinyl floor was stored in her memory after two and a half years of sharing the place with her sister.

"Do you miss it?"

Busted again. The nostalgia must have shown on her face. "Sure, I miss it. But I have a very nice kitchen at the apartment." Half the size, but nice.

"I'm sorry."

"Oh, don't be silly." Oriana waved away the apology. "It made sense for you and Cullen to take the house. I'm only one person. I don't need the space. I'll tell you what I really miss."

"What's that?"

"Jordan, of course!" She bent over and ruffled the dog's neck. She could have sworn he was grinning.

"You should get a dog."

Oriana straightened. "Yeah, you're right. I just don't think I have time for one right now. I feel like I'm starting to become a recluse with the afterschool program on top of all the time I need to spend on grading and lesson planning for my other classes every night."

"Do you wish you could quit the other classes?"

Oriana sighed and went to the sink to wash her hands. "You know me well."

"Too well." Nye tossed Oriana a teasing grin as she pulled a cheesecake out of the refrigerator.

"Those kids really need all the time and attention I can give them." Oriana dried her hands on a towel. "I think I could invest in them more if I didn't have to spend so much time and effort on the Language Arts classes."

"How are your kids doing?" Nye set the cake on the counter. "Everything okay since the fight?"

"Well … I'm glad you asked that."

"Uh-oh."

"You don't know it's bad."

"Sure." Nye leaned back against the counter and faced Oriana with her arms crossed.

Oriana wrinkled her nose. Sometimes having someone know her so well could be annoying. "Okay. For starters, Harry—"

"The principal?"

"Right. He told me today that, because of Dez's fight, I can't take the kids off of school grounds anymore."

"You're kidding." Nye's smirk dropped into a frown. "I'm so sorry." Her eyes widened. "The dance class …"

Oriana nodded. "Exactly. And the kids were just starting to get into it. I think they could get so much out of it if they could keep going."

"You don't have to sell me on the benefits of dance."

"I guess not." Oriana smiled and automatically opened the cabinet they had kept the plates in when she had shared the house with Nye. Dessert plates were still there, though they were different ones now since Oriana had taken hers to the apartment. "I was hoping you might be just as sold on continuing the lessons for the kids."

"What did you have in mind?" Nye opened the silverware drawer and pulled out the dessert forks.

"Could you come to the school and give them lessons? I think we could clear part of our classroom for it. Or maybe I could find a better space in one of the other rooms they're using for storage." Oriana bit her lip.

Nye's frown did not look like a "yes" was coming. "I'd love to, but I really don't see how I could fit it in. I have classes before and after yours. I wouldn't be able to drive there and back and still make my other classes. Could we do it in the evening?"

Oriana snorted. "A lot of the kids don't even show up for their mandatory afterschool hours. There's no way I'd get them to come at night."

"I'm sorry. You know I'd do it if I could."

"I know."

"Nicanor!" Nye said the word so sharply that Jordan sat up and looked at her.

"Nicanor?" Oriana stared at her sister's bright smile.

"Yes. I haven't assigned him any classes yet, so he'd be free to teach your kids."

Nicanor at her school? Just the thought was enough to make Oriana's heart all fluttery. "Do you think he would do it?"

"I think so. I know he wants to help out."

"Does he love kids?"

"Not exactly." Nye glanced away.

"He doesn't even like them, does he?" Oriana wasn't sure she liked Nye's sudden avoidance of eye contact.

"Well ... I don't think he's ever worked with them before."

"That's not an answer."

Nye met Oriana's gaze. "Do you want a dance instructor for your kids or not?"

"I want." Oriana couldn't help the grin that crept onto her face.

"Okay, then you take what you can get. You love kids enough for twenty adults anyway."

"Speaking of loving kids, I can't believe you're going to be a mom."

Nye's eyes widened as if she was apprehensive about the idea—an unusual expression to see on her face. "You're not the only one."

"I thought you said you were going to wait a few years before thinking about children."

"Yes, I did." She picked up the cheesecake. "Once again, God had other plans."

Judging from the twinkle in Nye's eyes and the smile she threw over her shoulder as the exited the kitchen, she was more than okay with this plan.

Oriana tried to ignore the cold wind as she ran on the sidewalk, her path lit by street lamps. The wind wasn't strong, but running into it increased its bite. She had to remember this was November and start wearing a scarf over her face for evening runs.

Tonight was probably just worse because she was running later than normal. She had felt a little tired by the time she got home after the late dinner at Nye and Cullen's, but she ate way too much of Nye's delicious pasta and cheesecake to even think of skipping her exercise. At times like this, she wished she had Nye's naturally slim figure—she didn't have to do a thing to keep her dancer's waif-like body. Of course, Nye didn't eat very much either.

Oriana blew out an extra heavy breath, trying to get her mind back on track. Thinking along those lines never did her mood any good. God had made the two sisters to be different, not clones. And He did it for a reason.

Oriana's attempt to be positive faltered as she turned the corner, puffing more than normal. Why did she feel so tired? Maybe she was just weary from how preoccupied her thoughts had been ever since dinner. Something was nagging at her mind, trying to squash her usually upbeat spirits. Why was she starting to freak out about her figure again? She hadn't envied Nye's skinniness for a long time.

She was jealous. The realization hit her so hard, she stopped running. She put her hands on her hips, breathing hard. The image of Nye and Cullen holding a new baby, watching him or her grow into a toddler, should have made Oriana happy, but for some reason it caused an ache in her chest.

Nye was her older sister. She should be the first to get married, have a family. But after three years of watching Nye treat men like a plague, Oriana had started to believe she would be the first, maybe the only one of the sisters to get married. After all, she had always been open to a relationship, even looking for one at times. How ironic that Nye would end up getting everything Oriana dreamed of.

God had other plans. Nye's eyes had been filled with such peace when she said the words.

Oriana started jogging again. She was being ridiculous. Of course God knew what He was doing. She needed to be patient and trust Him. Maybe she was just tired. Good thing she wouldn't have to work anymore tonight since it was Friday. She had the whole weekend to get everything done for Monday.

As she neared her apartment building, she slowed to a walk, tugging the hat off her sweaty hair.

A noise came from the bushes.

Oriana paused on the walkway that led to the building from the sidewalk. She looked around.

Nothing. The snow lining the path by the bushes didn't even look disturbed.

She shook her head at her skittishness and continued to the door. Those guys at the school must have rattled her more than she thought. Running at night may not be the safest thing to do, but she wasn't usually nervous about it. Her apartment was a closer distance to the school than the house she had shared with Nye while still keeping her just outside the rougher inner-city neighborhoods.

Still, she was relieved when she stepped inside and closed the door behind her.

"Running late again?"

Oriana jumped and turned to the voice.

It was only Mrs. Peters. The seventy-four-year-old woman stepped outside the open door to her apartment, her short orange-red dyed perm forming a perfect dome over her head. She crossed her arms and gave Oriana a firm stare, the creases on her forehead deepening. "I worry about you out there alone at night. It's just not safe."

Oriana smiled. "I'm careful, Mrs. Peters."

"If you ask me, you should stay inside. Does your mother know you run at night?"

"Yes, she does." If she hadn't already, she would have found out now from Mrs. Peters.

"If I know Caroline, she's not too happy about it."

Oriana gently touched Mrs. Peters's arm. "Thank you for caring so much about me. It makes me feel safer knowing you're looking out for me."

Mrs. Peters patted Oriana's hand, her tense lips softening into a smile. "You're a sweet young woman, Oriana."

"So are you."

Mrs. Peters laughed and waved Oriana away as she turned back to her apartment, the first one in the building.

"See you at church." Oriana headed for the staircase on

the left. She had discovered long ago that being genuinely grateful for the love church ladies like Mrs. Peters showed her was better than resenting their concern as intrusive. They meant well, and Oriana appreciated knowing that someone in the apartment building was a solid Christian, even if that also meant Oriana's mother had a built-in spy.

Oriana reached in her pocket for the key as she stopped at her door on the first landing. Why was she so startled when Mrs. Peters spoke to her? Something sure seemed wrong with her tonight. Maybe she could blame it on Nicanor. The sudden appearance of a handsome mystery man could throw any girl out of whack.

Oriana smiled at the excuse as she unlocked her apartment door. There was a light again, this time in the form of something happier to think about—even if it was only a silly schoolgirl crush.

Chapter Five

*"If I say, 'Surely the darkness shall cover me,
and the light about me be night,'
even the darkness is not dark to you;
the night is bright as the day,
for darkness is as light with you."*
– Psalm 139:11-12

Nicanor took a drag on a cigarette outside the studio's side entrance, as weary as if he had barely survived the weekend. He should be used to feeling tired. The eight hours guaranteed by sleeping pills were like a dead stupor that never refreshed him. They didn't prepare him for the Monday morning sun that was bright enough to blind a person. The snow on the ground wouldn't last much longer with the rays so intense.

The door opened a couple feet away from him, and Nye came outside. She spotted him by the side of the building and smiled. "Didn't your mother ever tell you to wear a jacket?" She directed a pointed look at his arms, bare beneath the short-sleeves of his T-shirt.

Had she? He didn't think he had even owned a jacket until he became an adult and went to America. He dropped the partially-smoked cigarette on the ground and stepped on it. "I don't remember." He had been so little. There was much he couldn't remember.

"I'm sorry, Nicanor … I forgot."

He stared at the pavement.

"You didn't have to put out the cigarette on my account."

"The habit isn't good."

"That's what Dante always said." She smiled.

He turned his head away to hide any sign of the inward pang that came with the memory.

"The sunlight looks so warm, but it's colder than I thought." Nye rubbed her sweater-clad arms with her hands. "Can we talk inside?"

He nodded. He reached the door first and held it for her as they entered.

She turned to face him as soon as they were inside the short passageway that was lined with costumes and dance gear she had collected for her students. "I have some good news I wanted to tell you."

"Yes?"

"Cullen and I are expecting."

Expecting what? He stared at her.

"A baby. We're going to have a baby." She smiled broadly.

He couldn't think of a word to say. It would not be Dante's baby. She was moving on. He forced himself to swallow. "Congratulations."

"Thanks. It's great timing for you to be here in case I need more help managing the studio as things progress. I wasn't going to ask you this before, but do you know how long you're going to stay?"

He felt the sudden pressure like a weight against his chest.

"Quite a while, I hope?" she added, as if thinking that would help.

"I ... I had not ... I have no plans."

"Oh, that's fine." She waved a hand to dismiss her question. "Forget I asked. I'm just so happy that you're going to take over some of those classes for me in the evenings, and I guess I was hoping it might be for a while. I should give you more time to get settled in before pressuring you like that. You don't even know if you like the job yet." She laughed at herself as she turned and went to the doorway that led onto the dance floor.

He breathed freely like a caged animal just let out of its prison. She probably hadn't meant to corner him. He would have answered her if he could, but he didn't know how long he would stay. He didn't know where he should go or what he should do. Only that he felt like he might be able to do something good here. Something to pay ...

Nye poked her head back through the doorway. "My students are arriving for class, but I needed to ask you a favor."

He braced himself.

"You remember that question I asked you the other day? About Oriana?"

Oriana. The name brought the image of her laughing eyes and sparkling grin, as bright as the sunshine outside.

Nye glanced behind her at the dance floor and the students he could hear entering. She stepped more fully into the hallway. "You never actually answered my question."

"What question?" As if he didn't know.

"If you would help her out."

Not sure what she meant, he just looked at her.

"It's not just for me," she continued, as if formulating an argument, "Oriana's class isn't allowed to come here anymore, and she very much wants them to continue with dance. I do, too, but I can't get to the school in the afternoon because of the classes here. Would you go there and teach the kids?"

The idea of trying to teach anything to a group of undisciplined ghetto kids, let alone dance, was nearly enough to make New York seem appealing. "You know how I teach?"

"Yes. A little toughness might do them some good." She smiled. "And Oriana will be there to balance things out."

"They have the facilities?"

"Well, Oriana thought she could find a room that would work."

Far from reassuring.

"Will you help her? Please?"

The request struck something inside him. Her eyes held earnest hope. She cared greatly about his answer. "Do *you* ask me?" If this help was for her, something she wanted, perhaps he could do it.

She blinked, looking surprised by the question. "You don't have to do it. Maybe you could give it a trial for a little while and see how it goes. I would really appreciate it, if you'd be willing."

"I'll do it."

She smiled.

There. A small payment on the debt. The weight on his heart told him this single favor wasn't enough to make a difference, but he had made her happy, at least for one moment. That was what Dante would want.

Oriana shook her head at her kids' scramble to grab their backpacks and dash out the door.

"Later!" Antonio and Brayden shouted in unison, as they sprinted away.

Oriana started to clear the books off the tables. She had to admit her students weren't the only ones glad that the day was over.

"Miss Sanders?"

Oriana turned to the small voice. LaTisha stood just inside the door, her eyes as wide as when she had to go through the spooky corridor.

"Want me to walk out with you?"

"No, that's okay."

Then what was the nervousness about?

LaTisha fiddled with a loose thread on the strap of her backpack, unconvincingly pretending to study it.

Oriana set the books on a table and went to the scared girl. "What is it, sweetie? Can I help?"

LaTisha turned those big orbs on her. "I don't wanna be no snitch."

"Okay." Oriana searched for the right words. "Are you worried about someone or something?"

She nodded. "Dez." LaTisha shyly dropped her gaze as soon as the word slipped out.

"Honey, it's okay." She smiled, relieved that LaTisha just wanted some girl talk. She had seen the way LaTisha followed Dez around when he'd let her. She wished LaTisha would idolize him a little less, but far be it from her to crush the girl's first puppy love. "You can talk to me about him, if you want."

LaTisha looked around, checking the room. "He's doing pot," she whispered.

Oriana's smile dropped. When would she ever stop expecting normal from these kids? She cleared her throat. "Have you seen him use it?"

LaTisha nodded gravely.

"More than once?"

Another nod. "My brother OD'd." The words were barely more than a whisper.

Oriana's heart ached that this little girl even knew what the term meant. Oriana had gone to the boy's funeral—another fifteen-year-old dead, from cocaine in that case. "Yes, I know. You did the right thing, LaTisha. You're looking out for Dez. I'm so proud of you." Oriana forced a smile of encouragement.

LaTisha's expression lightened a bit. She turned to go, then paused and looked back. "Will he get in trouble?"

"He'll get help. That's what he needs to make it through this."

"Okay," LaTisha said in a tiny, unsure voice as she left the room.

What a brave little girl. Tears welled in Oriana's eyes as she looked through the empty doorway into the dark hall where the light bulb flashed dimly. LaTisha could be cut off from her friends, maybe some of her family, if they knew what she had just done out of love for a boy. Oriana closed her eyes. Stop. Don't think about it. She had to get her mind on something other than all the horrible things that could happen to LaTisha if word got out.

It wouldn't get out. Oriana picked up the stack of books and shoved them in her bag. She would make sure no one knew LaTisha was her source, but she would also do what she promised—she would find a way to help Dez. First stop, Dez's mother.

With a firm set of her chin, Oriana barreled into the hallway and stopped.

A dark figure leaned against the wall near the stairs, one foot propped behind him.

That ridiculous bulb flickered above Oriana's head, making it impossible to see who the man was and probably very easy for him to see her. She walked out from under the light.

It looked like his head was turned toward her, but she couldn't see his face.

Reminding herself that security wouldn't have let him into the school unless he was okay, Oriana approached with more confidence. "May I help you?"

"I am to help *you*."

His foreign accent and cat-like grace as he straightened away from the wall could only be one person.

"Nicanor?" She was relieved, but her heart didn't seem to get the message. It felt like someone was having fun with a bouncy ball in her chest as she stopped a couple feet from him. "I didn't expect to see you here."

With a bandaged hand, he lowered the leather jacket he had held over his shoulder. "Nye asked me."

Alarm added another shot to her heart rate. "Is she okay? Did something happen?"

"No. Don't be afraid."

His voice, deep and smooth like she had imagined, was so

soothing—an effect that was negated when he looked directly at her with those electric blue eyes.

"Are all the children gone?"

"What?" The word sounded like a croak coming from her suddenly dry throat.

He looked away. "Your class. Are they gone?"

"Oh. Yes."

"Nye said you need help."

"She did?" Oriana blinked, trying to clear the fog from her mind. He was really going to think she needed help—mental help—at this rate.

"Dance classes. For the children."

"Oh, right." Heat rushed to her cheeks, making her actually thankful the hallway was so dark.

"You have a room?"

"You're going to teach it?" She couldn't help the smile that spread across her face. She was sure she was grinning from ear to ear.

He nodded, not meeting her gaze.

"Thank you so, so much. I can't tell you how much that means to me." Calm down. She made herself breathe evenly. She didn't need her crush turning into anything more because of gratitude.

"I owe much to Nye."

Right. He was only doing it because Nye asked him to. Good reminder. "Well, regardless, thank you."

"Will you show me the room?"

"Sure. It's down this way." She led him past her classroom and farther down the hall, trying not to get dreamy over Nicanor finally talking to her. She couldn't help feeling self-conscious that he was behind her as they went down the corridor. "Sorry it's so dark," she tossed over her shoulder for an excuse to check on him.

He was watching her, as she feared.

"Here it is." She stopped at a closed door with paper covering the inside of the window. She tried the knob. "It's locked, but I have a key." She set her book bag down and scrounged around in her purse for her keys. Why did she have to carry such a big purse anyway?

"Got it!" she exclaimed to hide her nerves as her fingers closed over the elusive keys. She resisted the urge to sigh with relief when she managed to insert the correct key into the knob on the first try and expertly unlocked the door. She swung it open for Nicanor.

He gestured for her to go in first.

Ah, chivalry. Must be an Argentine thing. Oriana went inside and cringed at the stacks of dust-covered boxes that cluttered the room along with miscellaneous items: an old projector on a stand, a table leaning against the wall next to a few folded, rusted chairs like the ones in her classroom. She looked at Nicanor for his reaction but couldn't read anything in his expression, as usual.

This Shadow

He just surveyed the room with those intense eyes.

"It used to be a teacher's lounge. I think. I know it's a mess, but it has the most open space of any of the rooms on this floor. At least it will once we clean it out."

A slight eyebrow raise was her only response, as he drew the toe of his shoe along the dirty wooden floor.

Her cheeks warmed as she realized what he might have thought she meant. "I mean the kids and I, of course. We'll clean it out."

Was that a twitch at the corner of his mouth? She wouldn't mind being laughed at if it meant he would smile.

He glanced at her with his typical brooding expression instead. "It will work."

She smiled. "Awesome! When do you want to start?"

"Cleaning up?"

Was he making a joke? She stared at him, but still couldn't tell, especially when he wouldn't look at her. Was it possible he had a sense of humor somewhere behind that shadowed face? "No," she said cautiously, "I meant the class, actually. Nye usually did once a week on Thursdays, but we can do any day you'd like."

"Thursday."

"Okay. Great." Two days to get the room ready. Not impossible, but definitely daunting. She put on a smile and noticed the bandage wrapped around his hand. "Did you hurt yourself?"

"Not much." He abruptly turned and headed for the door.

"Oh, sorry." She hurried after him. "Didn't mean to pry. I suppose you need to get going. I do, too, actually. I have to see a student's mother a little ways from here. On Henry Street, I think." She closed the door behind them and locked it. She was blabbering again, an annoying nervous habit she must do something about.

"By Third Street?"

She turned to catch him watching her before he quickly looked away from her gaze. "I think so."

"Rough part of town."

"Yes, I know. So is this."

"There is safety here."

He must be referring to the security guards and metal detectors. Kids could unfortunately get dangerous people and things through anyway. "I have gone off campus before."

"Alone?"

"Well ... yes." Was he actually concerned about her?

He looked directly at her for a moment. "You shouldn't go alone."

Wow. He was. That annoying heat flushed her cheeks again, but she managed to keep her mouth from hanging open. "I—" she squeaked. She cleared her throat. "I'll be fine. But thank you."

"I'll go with you."

This Shadow

Her mouth dropped open. She closed it. The image of Nicanor sitting next to her in her tiny car made her heart race with nothing short of panic. And a bit of a thrill. "That's very kind, but … I'll really be okay."

"I will go with you." He gave her a stare that was more like a glower—annoyance and all.

My, he could look scary. "Okay. My car's out front." The flight of butterflies in her stomach turned into a full-fledged migration as Oriana started down the hallway to the stairs. She was keenly aware of Nicanor's presence beside her, even with a couple feet between them. She hoped she got over her thing for Nicanor in a hurry. This puppy love stuff was for the dogs.

***

Nicanor waited while Oriana spoke to what seemed like the fifteenth person they had met on their way to the street at the back of the school. Her fan club was mostly children but also included plenty of teachers, male and female. They all had one thing in common—they were happier after talking to Oriana.

Her perkiness was apparently contagious to most people, though she also grew serious for two adults who spoke to her with grim faces and hushed voices. Nicanor had known someone else like that once—someone able to be exactly what everyone needed. She had always known how to be what Nicanor needed. Even when he pushed her away in his boyish anger, she came back. Except for the one time when she could not. When his father screamed that she was gone.

"Sorry about that." Oriana's smile interrupted Nicanor's thoughts as she approached and pointed past him. "My car's just down there."

He looked where she pointed and picked out a little red Beetle behind a black car. For the second time that day and in years, he came close to smiling. The Beetle had to be hers.

"Sorry." She watched his reaction as they walked to the car. "It's pretty small."

She apologized more than anyone he had met. She went around to the driver's side and unlocked her door, as he stopped by the passenger side, shrugging into the jacket he had been carrying.

"Aren't you cold in that?" She gave his thin jacket a look across the roof of the car. "We need to get you some serious winter gear for these parts." She held up a hand clad in a bright red mitten to make her point.

The cuteness of the gesture unbelievably made him want to smile again. Too bad he had forgotten how. He tried to open the door instead. Locked.

"Sorry," came another apology, as Oriana dove into the car. "I have to unlock that door by hand." The window muffled her voice as she stretched across the seat to reach the inside lock of the passenger door.

He opened it and got in while she tossed a bag in the back.

"It's an older model. New for me, though. My old car got totaled last year."

Was she always this talkative? As she took off her mitten and put the key in the ignition, he thought her fingers trembled. He often made people tense, and he usually didn't care—it made them keep their distance. But the idea of Oriana getting nervous around him didn't sit well. "It's perfect." He hoped the truthful statement might help her to relax.

She gave him a quick glance, as if startled, then looked out the windshield. "Thank you." She checked the mirrors and backed up the car. "So, what do you think of Harper?" She switched gears and checked the mirror as she pulled out onto the street.

He was dreading this part. The small talk. But he couldn't have let her go alone. Nye would have even more to forgive if he let something happen to her sister. "It's normal. Some good, some bad."

"I'd say that's exactly right. When I grew up in Harper, I thought the city was all good. I didn't even know about the Projects across the river. I guess our parents kept us away from it. It's like a whole different world here from the one I grew up in, even though it's all in the same city."

Good. Being with a talker had advantages—he might not have to say a word.

"What about you? Where did you grow up? I've heard Argentina is beautiful. Did you like it?"

So much for not talking. How was he supposed to answer three questions at a time?

"Sorry. I have a bad habit of asking a bunch of questions at once. I got it from my mother." She bit her lip, then let it go. "Nye doesn't do that." She turned the wheel to make a turn. "I'll narrow it down to one." A smile banished the lines on her brow. "Where did you grow up?"

He thought a moment, not wanting to answer, but he found himself replying before he decided to. "Buenos Aires."

"Was it good or bad?"

"For some, good." He hoped she would stop there.

"But what was it like for you?"

He looked out the window at the decaying buildings they passed, luxury apartments compared to the slums he could still see in his mind and feel in his heart. "Not good."

"I'm sorry."

"Some things are not yours to apologize."

Her profile looked so peaceful as she kept her eyes fixed on the road. The corner of her mouth pulled up. "No, but I'm still sorry." She looked at him for a moment, and he turned his head away.

She had too much compassion in her eyes. Sometimes compassion, sometimes joy. Always too much. Too much life and too much like the eyes he wished he could see again. The color was different, but the innocent love they held for everyone was the same.

"I bet living in New York was fun." Oriana watched the road again. "So much activity and energy. Always something to do. Do you miss it?"

"No."

"Oh." She blinked. "Will you go back?"

A question he hadn't even asked himself. "You ask many questions."

"Sorry." She cringed, as she drove the car up to a curb between two parked vehicles. The Beetle was small enough that she could get away with not backing in to parallel park. "I think this is it." With the car still running, Oriana ducked down to see the apartment building through the passenger window. "Not too pretty, huh?"

It looked nearly identical to the place Nicanor was staying.

"If you'd like to wait in the car, that'd be fine." She straightened and looked at Nicanor, who avoided her gaze by pretending interest in the building. "This is where Dez lives— you know the boy you pulled out of the fight the other day? I need to see his mother about something serious he may have gotten into. She hasn't been willing to come to the school in the past, so I'm not sure what kind of reception I'll get."

Nicanor glanced at her.

She still watched him. "It might not be pleasant."

He looked out the window. Two hoods kept an eye on the car while they smoked joints near the entrance to the building. A group of teenagers, their breath making puffs in the cold air that matched the smokers, hung out at the bottom of the stairs, also staring at the newcomers. "I'll go."

"Okay." Oriana's tone sounded skeptical, or was it disappointed?

Nicanor didn't want to annoy her, but watching Oriana go out there alone would be like watching a lamb find her way to the slaughter. He opened his door and got out as she rounded the car.

"Hi."

He nearly started when Oriana spoke to the teens by the stairs, shining that bright smile on them. The three boys looked like they didn't know how to react while the girl answered with a short nod.

"Cold day to be outside, huh?" Oriana said, as she and Nicanor started up the stairs.

He hoped she realized she was not going to get an answer. She seemed so determined to be cheerful that he was afraid she might try to chat with the smokers at the top of the stairs.

The two men ogled Oriana as she walked up. Nicanor didn't like the thoughts reflected in their eyes.

Oriana innocently directed her smile at them when she got closer, but Nicanor swiftly stepped between them and her. He gently held her elbow to guide her toward the door.

She glanced up at him, startled.

"Hey, hot mama." One of the men gave her a disgusting grin. "What's your hurry?"

Nicanor pinned him with a hard glare.

He held up his hands and took a step back. "Easy, man. We're cool."

Nicanor opened the door, the security lock not surprisingly out of order, and ushered Oriana inside. Maybe he was overreacting, even if they were smoking crack. This was only Harper, as the hood's quick back-down made plain.

"Thanks." Oriana paused briefly inside the door and looked at him.

It was an ordinary thing. He deserved no thanks for it.

She passed the staircase to go down the hallway. "Though I'm not sure it was necessary. I don't think they meant any harm."

Nicanor followed behind, marveling at her innocence. Was she purposefully lying to herself, or was she really that naïve?

"Dez lives in apartment twelve." She glanced over her shoulder at him. "At least that's the address his mother gave the school."

They turned a corner into another hallway and passed a few more apartments.

A loud slam came from behind a closed door.

Oriana started, then laughed softly at herself. "Wow, I'm jumpy lately." Amusement still played on her lips when she reached number twelve and stopped.

A baby cried inside the apartment while other children yelled, either to be heard over the noise or to make some of their own.

"Well, here goes." With a glance at Nicanor, Oriana raised her fist and knocked. Hard.

Nicanor raised his eyebrows at the loud rap. Could the schoolteacher be hiding some force under that sweet exterior?

The door opened a crack and the crying grew much louder, as if right by the door. Someone's eye filled the crevice below Oriana's height. "What." The unfriendly voice sounded female.

"Hi, I'm Dez's teacher, Oriana Sanders." Oriana's tone was as confident and chipper as her smile.

"He ain't here."

"I'm here to see his mother. Is she home?"

The door opened farther, swung by a girl of no more than thirteen with a streak of purple through her black hair. She held the sobbing baby, face wet and nose running, on her barely-defined hip. The infant slipped down as she watched them, and she had to heft him higher again, bending sideways to create a place to set him on. "Yeah, she's here. You can come in, I guess."

"What a sweetie," Oriana cooed at the baby as they entered the room.

An old TV sat on a stand next to the wall by the door. Some hospital drama played out on the screen as two small children sat in front of it, staring at the TV as if the show was the only real world.

Nicanor couldn't blame them. The run-down apartment, sparsely furnished with a sofa and chairs that looked like they had come from a garbage dump and the stained, worn carpeting the children sat on were symbols of a world that needed to be escaped.

The children didn't look at the visitors or move to make room for them by the door, which meant Nicanor and Oriana had two feet to stand in unless they went around the hypnotized kids.

He looked at Oriana and blinked.

Somehow, she had already taken the baby in her arms and was dabbing its tears and wet nose with a tissue. There must be no age requirement for her magical personality—the baby forgot to cry while staring at her face and reached tiny fingers to touch her nose.

Oriana laughed and glanced at Nicanor.

His breath caught. Did she know how beautiful she looked at that moment? No, she was nothing like the self-obsessed models and dancers he used to date. Maybe that was her magic.

Even the teenager who had prematurely developed frown lines on her forehead smiled at the sight of her baby sibling cooing at Oriana. "Dez talks about you," she announced, apparently intending a compliment.

"Raquelle?" A woman's voice came from the connected

room. "What happened to Sammy?"

"Nothing," Raquelle yelled back. "Dez's teacher is here."

The mother hustled into the room, curls of dark shiny hair bobbing alongside her weary face. "You Ms. Sanders?" She directed a look at Oriana as she crossed the room to pick up a jacket from the torn sofa.

"Yes." Oriana smiled over the baby's head. "I'm so pleased to finally meet you."

"Sorry, honey, but I just ain't got time." The woman looked to be only a few years older than Oriana, but the deep creases on her face, like her daughter's, showed that life had taken a heavy toll. "I'm working the late shift at the store."

She put a hand on each of the TV watchers' heads as she passed them. "Raquelle, take the baby back and let Ms. Sanders go."

Raquelle hefted Sammy from Oriana as her mother brushed past and went out the door.

"Wait, please!" Oriana rushed after her.

Nicanor caught up with a few steps, then followed a short distance behind as Oriana walked alongside the mother.

"I need to speak with you about Dez."

"What about him?"

"I'm afraid he's in trouble."

The woman laughed as she rounded the corner. "Honey, ain't that why he in detention?"

"It's more of an afterschool program now."

"Uh-huh. Well, he promised me he tryin' harder to stay in school."

"Yes, and I believe he was." Oriana's long stride let her easily keep up with the shorter woman's fast clip. "But lately his attitude and his behavior are getting worse."

"I can't do your job for you. I don't have no problems making him mind at home."

"I'm sure you don't." Oriana didn't sound the least bit offended. "But I'm not here to talk about his behavior. There's something more serious that I just learned."

The mother kept marching toward the front door.

"I believe he's using marijuana."

So Oriana did know. Maybe she wasn't quite as naïve as Nicanor thought.

The mother stopped by the door and turned to Oriana, her mouth in a hard line. "My boys don't do drugs, Ms. Sanders. That's the one thing I won't allow, and they know it."

"I believe you won't allow it." Oriana stood in front of her. "But what if he's doing it without your knowledge? If you could just talk to him, or take a look at his eyes. His mood swings—"

"That's enough of that, teacher." The woman's eyes narrowed. "You got no idea what it's like here, so don't go tellin' me how to be a mother to my kid." She yanked the door open and walked out.

Oriana started to follow. "That's not what—" She stopped outside the door, spotting the two hoods from before, now at the bottom of the stairs. She glanced at Nicanor as he came and stood beside her. "Sorry. That didn't go as I hoped."

Of all people, Oriana did not need any forgiveness. "Your only guilt is you care too much." He watched the two men as he spoke. "For that, no apologies."

"Thank you, Nicanor." Her smile reappeared.

They started down the stairs.

She looked at him. "Can I drive you to your place?"

"No, I'll walk."

She stopped on the sidewalk and turned to face him. "You live near here?"

"Third Street."

"Oh." She dropped her gaze for a second, too late to hide the surprised widening of her eyes. "Are you sure you won't get cold in that jacket?"

"Yes." Teaching kids must have developed her mothering instincts.

"Okay. Thanks for being my bodyguard." She angled her eyes to the side to indicate the men behind her.

"They're leaving."

She looked back as they went the other direction on the sidewalk. "I guess you scared them off." She faced him again, her eyes twinkling.

Such happiness. Was that what life was like without guilt? Without regrets?

He turned and walked away. He could not risk her magic on him. It might work, but it would be wrong for anyone so guilty to be happy.

Jerusha Agen

Chapter Six

*"He uncovers the deeps out of darkness
and brings deep darkness to light."*
– Job 12:22

"I know it's true." Oriana lowered her voice and moved closer to the wall as kids rushed down the hallway, bursting with the release from their last classes of the day. "I've thought he was ... on something for a while. I just needed more evidence."

"Which you still don't have." Harry looked at his watch. "Look, I have a meeting today, but if you want to stop by my office tomorrow before your class, I might have time to discuss it more."

He glanced at the children who gave him a wide berth as they hurried past. "You can use the old teachers' lounge for your dance class for now if you can find somewhere to move all the junk in there. But it's only on a trial basis. And we'll have to get this instructor approved, as well."

She opened her mouth to speak, but he stopped her with his famous raised finger.

"As for the other problem, unless you have something

more than a rumor, we can't do anything about it." He checked his watch again. "I have to go. Have a good class."

Harry brushed by Oriana as she mulled over his words. "We *can* do something about it," she muttered to herself as she started to move against the flow of the kids to head upstairs. "We have to."

"What, Miss Sanders?"

Oriana looked to see LaTisha fall in step beside her. "Oh, I didn't see you there." Oriana smiled. *Lord, please don't let her ask about Dez.* There wasn't any good news to share. "How was science today?" Oriana tried to ignore the twinge of guilt from intentionally attempting to distract her student.

"Okay, I guess. Still don't like it."

"But you're doing better in it anyway. I knew you could."

"Uh-huh." LaTisha sounded unaffected by the encouragement, but Oriana caught the brightness in her eyes and the small upturn of her lips. "Mr. Williams told us about a museum around here." LaTisha tugged on the shoulder strap of her backpack as they started up the stairs. "Do you know about it?"

"You mean the Children's Science Museum?"

"I guess." She shrugged—a cute attempt to act casual.

"Yes, I've been there. It's really wonderful."

"Can we go?"

Oops. Should have seen that one coming. Oriana took a moment to choose her words as they reached the landing and tackled the next flight of stairs. "Well, I'm afraid our class won't be going anywhere away from school for a while."

"Why not?"

"Because of what happened at Mrs. Chandler's dance studio the other day."

"Oh." LaTisha stopped and sucked in a breath. She faced Oriana, eyes wide. "You mean we have to quit dance lessons?"

"Oh, honey, no." Oriana stopped walking. If only she were free to calm the little girl with a hug. "We have a new teacher who's going to come here to the school to teach you. Isn't that fantastic?"

LaTisha's furrowed brow was not the positive reaction Oriana expected. "A new teacher? Not Mrs. Chandler anymore?"

Poor LaTisha. She still had the Nye-like bun in her hair. Oriana smiled gently. "Maybe she'll be able to come in some days." Oriana would have to see what she could do about that. "But she sent us one of her friends who is a professional dancer from New York City. Mr. Pessoa. Mrs. Chandler says he's an even better dancer than she is." Oriana hoped her effort at enthusiasm would be contagious and prayed that Nicanor was still going to show up. After his sudden departure the evening before, she wasn't sure if he intended to come back.

"Okay." LaTisha trudged up the stairs, a frown still sagging her mouth.

Oriana was battling a sudden onslaught of sad thoughts

herself. The idea that she might not see Nicanor again was a challenge to her hallmark ability to think positively about everything. In fact, the thought was downright depressing. Still, she couldn't let that distract her from taking advantage of the moment to speak with LaTisha. "I've been wanting to talk to you about Maria. I think you might really like her, if you give her a chance."

LaTisha turned her head away but not before Oriana caught the flash in her eyes. "Don't want to."

"I really think you're missing out. She's one of the coolest girls I know."

LaTisha sneaked a glance at Oriana.

Good, she was curious anyway. "And it would be a real sign of maturity if you would help her out. She's pretty scared of you and the other kids, you know. Maybe you could just say 'hi' sometime. What do you think?"

LaTisha looked at Oriana as she continued to march up the stairs. "That what Jesus wants me to do?"

Oriana tried to hide her shock. Maybe LaTisha had been paying attention those few Sundays. "Definitely."

"Is he nice?"

"Jesus?"

"The new dance teacher."

Ah, the rapid changes of the young mind. The image of Nicanor's brooding face did not bring up "nice" as a first descriptor, unless she was talking about his looks. After his heroic insistence on protecting her yesterday, though, Oriana was starting to believe that what she had told herself to defend her crush might be right after all—the foreboding exterior was hiding a good guy underneath. "Yes. He's nice." She smiled at herself and the flush that heated her face. She was relieved she taught kids who were too young to notice such things.

"Miss Sanders?" LaTisha spoke up as they finally reached the top of the last stairs.

"Yes?"

"Are you blushing?"

Right. And just how in the world could LaTisha see that in the dim lighting? "My face might be red from climbing all these stairs. I'm getting hot, aren't you?" It wasn't a lie. She was getting warm, though she didn't really think stair climbing was the cause. For once, it would be a relief that LaTisha would be distracted by her usual fear of the dark hallway in a few seconds.

"No, I'm not hot." LaTisha cheerfully headed right into the hallway, not hesitating a moment.

Oriana moved slowly forward on autopilot and watched as LaTisha's walk picked up a little skip, though she aimed for the dim light bulb, flashing as usual.

LaTisha stopped under it and turned back to her teacher. "The people light." She grinned, pointing up at the bulb.

"That's right." Oriana didn't think she could possibly smile any bigger as she watched LaTisha skip through the open door of the classroom. Thank the Lord for that little girl. There was no better feeling than finding out a student had actually taken to heart something she had tried to teach them. There was nothing like seeing a light begin to shine.

Speaking of light … The glow from an open doorway farther down the hallway caught her eye. No one was supposed to be in any of those rooms.

She reached her classroom and looked inside.

Jonique and LaTisha sat at a table, the only arrivals so far.

"You two wait in here. I'll be right back."

"Whatever," Jonique answered with a loud pop of her chewing gum.

Oriana turned away from the door, holding her tongue for the moment. An intruder was more important than dealing with Jonique's "whatever" attitude just then. Oriana cautiously approached the light. As she got closer, she realized it was spilling out of the room Nicanor had approved for their dance classes.

She was probably being silly, Oriana told herself, trying to calm the wild ideas that came to her mind to explain the light. It could be Harry inside. He had a key, of course.

He also had a meeting. A noise, like something scraping across the floor, made her jump. She stopped just short of the door, staying close to the wall. "The Lord is my shepherd," she whispered to herself. She took a deep breath and stepped in front of the door.

A man in a black T-shirt and jeans bent over a huge box, his shiny black hair reflecting the overhead fluorescent lights.

The flutter in her stomach identified him as fast as her eyes did. "Nicanor?"

He straightened and glanced at her, apparently not startled at all. Locks of his hair fell forward more than usual. He pushed the thick hair back, revealing droplets of sweat glistening on his forehead.

She wondered how many times he would leave her searching for her voice. "I didn't know," she cleared her throat, "if I'd even see you again."

"I said I would teach."

"Yes, you did." Nye had assured her, when Oriana called last night to talk about Nicanor's behavior, that he was often just abrupt. That he would be back. But Oriana couldn't shake the fear that he might not. Fear for the children's sake, of course. "I'm sorry. I didn't mean to distrust you."

He looked right at her, and she felt the jolt of those electric eyes. "You apologize too much."

She smiled. She didn't know why. Maybe because the statement was the first personal comment she had ever heard him make. It might not be a flattering one, but she'd take it.

His eyebrows dipped as he watched her reaction.

Was it a good thing that she seemed to confuse him? At least he was dropping his guard a little, which allowed her to read him better. "Well, as long as I can forgive just as much, it's not so bad, right?"

He looked away, a frown pulling at his lips.

Blew it again. She still had no clue how she always ended up saying the wrong thing to him.

He rested his right hand on his hip.

The bandage was gone, and she thought she could see scratches on the backs of his fingers. "No bandage?"

"Fast healer."

"You're also a magician."

He raised an eyebrow.

"I thought I had locked the door to this room."

"Maybe not." His gaze fixed on something behind her.

"You okay, Miss Sanders?" Dez's voice startled her. He stood in the doorway, watching Nicanor suspiciously while LaTisha, Jonique, and Antonio shoved in beside him to see.

Her heart warmed at Dez's show of bravado for her sake, especially after their talk just the day before. "Yes, Dez, I'm fine. I thought I told you girls to stay in the classroom."

"Why?" Jonique snapped her gum, looking Nicanor up and down like a woman of the world far beyond her twelve years. "He dangerous?"

"No." His effect on her emotions didn't count. "He's your new dance teacher, Mr. Pessoa. Mr. Pessoa," she looked at Nicanor whose aloof aura was back at full strength, "these are some of my students. Dez, Antonio, LaTisha, and Jonique." She pointed to each one as she rattled off their names. "And

This Shadow

Juan," she added, spotting the boy's dark brown hair appear behind the others.

Dez stepped into the room and turned so that Juan was in front of him. Dez's gaze bounced between Juan and Nicanor. Oriana's heart squeezed at the tactics such a young boy thought he needed for survival. "Well, since most of us are here already, why don't we give Mr. Pessoa a hand?"

"With what?" Dez's momentarily helpful spirit was already banished like an unwelcome visitor.

"This," Oriana spread her arms wide to encompass the room, "is going to be our new dance floor!"

The kids stared at the cluttered, grimy room.

"For real?" Antonio's disbelief reflected in his eyes.

"For real. But we have to clean it up first. Dez, you and Antonio start with those boxes over there." She pointed at the stacks as she spoke. "We'll move most of them to the hallway for now. Jonique, go get the broom from our classroom, please. Juan and LaTisha, you two can work on taking those chairs out into the hall."

LaTisha and Dez shot Oriana startled glances.

"Come on. Let's get to it." Oriana smiled innocently. "The room won't clean itself." The kids would get used to it. She figured two months into the year was long enough for her to begin her anti-segregation program with them. Their racial and gang tensions were strong, but, if she started slowly, she hoped to at least get them to see that their "enemies" were just kids who were a lot like themselves.

"You don't have to do this."

She started at Nicanor's voice close behind her. She turned toward him, trying not to get silly because of his proximity. "It's good for them." She kept her voice lowered. "Besides, I never meant for you to clean the room at all, let alone by yourself."

"It's no trouble."

"I hope not, because I can't have the kids do this for their whole class. I shouldn't anyway." She smiled. "They have some homework we have to get to. Now I want you to promise you won't work on this anymore by yourself until I can help you after the kids go home. Deal?" Without thinking, she put out her hand for him to shake.

He looked at her hand. "No deal."

She started to pull her hand back when he suddenly took it. His skin felt so warm on hers, his hold gentle, but firm, like the power of muscles barely held in check.

He met her gaze. "I promise I will not finish without you."

She knew from the rush of heat that her face was probably beet red, but she was more concerned with breathing at the moment. Not the kind of reaction she was supposed to have to a man she shouldn't be interested in. She managed a wobbly smile. "Thanks." Now she was the one who looked away as she drew back her hand, trying not to notice how cold it felt out of his grasp.

Oriana looked up just in time to see Dez headed for the classroom door. "Dez, will you stay a minute, please?"

He stopped, reluctance obvious in the sullen glare and clenched jaw. The always-present chip on his shoulder was perfectly balanced on his defiant, arms-crossed stance.

Oriana waited until Brayden, the last student to leave, disappeared out the doorway, then turned her full attention to Dez. She took a breath to start, but he jumped in first—

"My sister says you talked to my mom." Anger glinted in his still-red eyes.

"Yes, I did. I'm concerned about you."

"You got no right to do that."

"To talk to your mother?"

His head jerked in a tight nod.

"I didn't mean to go behind your back. You're changing, Dez. You're falling farther behind in school. Your teachers tell me you're acting up in classes more, and I've seen how you're treating the other kids."

"It's my life."

So young to start using that catch-all excuse. Tired of her own lecture, she pulled out a chair by the table nearest the door and turned it to face Dez. She sat down a couple feet away from him. A new approach was in order. "So you're mad at me for talking to your mom."

He shifted his jaw, not looking at her.

"Then why were you still ready to defend me today, when you thought I was in danger?"

He shoved his hands in his jeans pockets and shrugged.

She waited.

He finally looked at her, the anger fading from his eyes. "You're a nice lady, Miss Sanders, but you gotta stay out of my business."

She wondered how many times he had heard his older brother use that phrase. "I can't do that if you're in trouble. Your life is worth far too much."

He dropped his gaze to the floor, his lower lip protruding in a way that painfully reminded Oriana of how young he was.

"If you can give me a straight answer to one question, I'll consider it."

He lifted his head.

"Are you using?"

His eyes widened slightly as he stared at her for a second. He jerked away and headed for the door as quickly as his swaggering stride would allow, brushing past Nicanor on his way out.

Nicanor took a few steps into the room, watching Oriana.

She had forgotten for a moment that Nicanor was still in

the building—a testament to how great her concern was for Dez. "Did you hear that?"

He nodded.

Frustration suddenly bubbled up inside her. Was it a male gender requirement to never talk in a conversation? She stood and shoved in the chair, then went around the tables, performing the usual clean-up ritual with jerking motions.

"I know he's using." She snatched up the books and pencils. "And he knows I know. But I can't do a thing about it."

"You don't have to."

She stopped, holding a stack of books in her arms, and stared at Nicanor. "He's twelve years old, and he's on marijuana, maybe even coke. You think that's okay?" Her voice twisted with a mixture of incredulity and irritation.

"His trouble is here." He touched his forehead. "And here." He tapped his chest, over the heart. "You can't change it."

She opened her mouth, then closed it, not sure how to respond. If she didn't know better, she'd say he sounded like a Christian. Was he going to tell her next that only God can change people's hearts? She needed the reminder.

She pushed the books into the bag and shook her head at herself. She gave Nicanor a small smile. "You're right. I'm sorry to take out my frustration on you. I just don't want to use that as an excuse to do nothing. I want to help."

His blue eyes looked right into hers. Did he see her doubts and worries reflected there? "You help them much."

The corner of her mouth tugged up at the phrasing. She loved his little idiosyncrasies with language, the charming word choice and inflections that showed he wasn't a native English speaker. Careful, she reminded herself, love is a strong word.

"Thank you." She hoisted the purse strap over her shoulder and picked up the book bag. "Speaking of helping, I'm supposed to finish up our little dance studio. Were you able to get much more done after we left you alone?" She headed for the doorway, and he stepped aside to let her through first.

"Much."

She imagined she saw a glimmer of humor in his eyes as she passed by him. She couldn't be certain the inscrutable man was joking, so she held in a laugh and just smiled as they walked toward the light pouring from the dance room. "Sorry if we were in the way. You did leave some of the work for me, right? You promised you would."

"Of course." He stopped at the doorway and gestured with a sweep of his arm that she should go in first.

Her mouth dropped open at the sight of the completely cleared room. Nicanor had even moved a row of shelves that had split the space in half to now line a wall at one end of the room. "Wow. What did you do with all the stuff?"

"The room next door."

"Great. That works." Exactly what she was going to do with it, though she didn't know if it would all fit in there. "Thank you so much."

He looked away.

"I can't believe all the work you did. But you were supposed to leave some of it for me."

He went to the doorway and picked up the broom that leaned against the wall there. He walked to Oriana. "You can sweep." He held out the broom to her.

"Thanks." Oriana wrinkled her nose with a smile as she reached for the broom. Her fingers accidentally brushed Nicanor's as she grabbed the wooden handle and a jolt passed through her. It's winter, she told her girlish romantic self. Static electricity is a beast.

She cleared her suddenly dry throat and turned away. "You don't have to stay." She walked over to the window and dropped her book bag and purse next to it. She started sweeping a random patch of the floor. "I'll finish this, and then we'll be ready for tomorrow." She felt him watch her for what felt like forever but was probably only a second or two.

He silently headed for the door.

She stopped sweeping and looked to see him pick up his jacket from one of the folding chairs that remained in the room. "See you tomorrow?"

He nodded without facing her completely. "If you wish."

He was out the door and gone before Oriana could process

his almost *Princess Bride* response. She hoped he meant "yes," but she really had no idea what he meant. She had not been exaggerating when she called him mysterious.

She started to sweep again, not minding a bit that her work took her back in the direction of the window. Unlike in her classroom, this window faced the front of the school and should offer a nice view of anyone leaving. That is, if the glass wasn't so filthy. She frowned at the smudges that blocked her view. She propped the broom against the wall and undid the latches that locked the window in place.

Her first heft did nothing. She tried again. With a grunt, she managed to produce a crack and then slowly slid up the curmudgeonly window a good five inches before it jammed again. She leaned over, blinking into the cold air that blew in as she peered through the opening. Maybe she would still be able to see him.

Not a chance. Only part of the street and the far side of the sidewalk were visible from her vantage point. She'd have to shove her whole head out to be able to see anything closer to the building. Without giving herself time to think about how childish she was being, she started to attempt to fit her head through.

Her cell phone rang, causing her to jerk and hit her head on the window.

"Ow." She pulled back in and rubbed the sore spot on her head. She reached in her bag and found her ringing phone.

"Hello?"

"Hi, sweetheart, it's Mom."

"Hi, Mom." Despite her current discomfort, Oriana had to smile at her mom's habit of announcing her identity, as if her daughter wouldn't recognize the voice.

"How are you? How's your day? Everything going well?"

"It's a little painful at the moment, but …" Irrationally annoyed with the window, Oriana put her shoulder against it and attempted to shove it further open.

"Painful? Are you okay?"

"Yeah, I'm fine." She grunted as she pushed.

"You don't sound fine. Is everything okay?"

"Hah!" The window released and flew to its maximum opening height.

"Honey?"

"Sorry, Mom." Oriana blinked at the strong, cold wind that rushed inside. "I was just trying to get a window open."

"Oh."

"What were you calling about?" Now Oriana could see the front of the building and the closer sidewalk if she leaned out.

"The Thanksgiving menu."

Nicanor would be long gone by now. Oh, well. God knew best. No sense humoring a schoolgirl crush.

"Should we keep it the same or try to change it this year?"

"Mom, you know you never like to change it. Every time Nye or I have suggested any new dish, you always have some reason why you don't think we should make it."

"I'm open to trying new things. You've just never suggested anything that's appropriate."

"Right." Oriana smiled as she continued looking out. She was getting cold without her jacket. She looked up at the portion of the window she had worked so hard to open. Now what if she couldn't get it closed again?

"Well, I'm sorry if you think it needs to be changed. I always thought you liked our traditions."

"Mom, don't be silly. Of course I do. Honestly, I wouldn't change a thing about the menu."

"You're sure?"

"Yes, I'm sure. It's all of my favorite foods." She reached her free hand for the window and tried to pull it down. Great. It was stuck.

"Well, good. I'll talk to Nye and see what she thinks."

"Okay." Oriana cringed with humor. Nye was the proponent of trying new dishes for Thanksgiving, but, so far, their mother had always won out. Thank the Lord they were at least getting along better these days. "I have to go, Mom, but tell me if you need me to bring anything, okay?"

"All right. You have a good evening. And be careful leaving that school. I worry about you there."

"I know, but God's not going to let anything happen to me. I'll be fine. You have a good night, too."

Oriana smiled as she tucked her cell phone back into her

purse. For the first time since the death of Dante, it promised to be a very happy Thanksgiving. She grabbed the window with both hands this time, but stopped as she caught sight of movement across the street.

Was that Dez? There was no mistaking the blue jacket and red baseball cap, slightly askew. What was he still doing at school? He stood with another boy behind the cars parked on that side of the street, but Oriana could still see them thanks to the third floor height.

Dez and the other boy looked around, as if making sure they weren't being watched, before the boy handed Dez some folded bills. Dez reached in his pocket and pulled out a little bag of white …

Oriana didn't have to be any closer to know what was in it. She spun away from the window and sprinted down the hall. She trotted down the stairs as fast as she could. The main hallway was empty as she ran to the front of the building.

"I'll be back," she gasped to Bill, the security guard, as she rushed by. She launched through the doors, not stopping until she reached the street.

They were gone.

Oriana jogged across the street to make sure.

A boy in a red cap walked on the sidewalk far away, almost out of sight.

"Dez!" Oriana yelled.

He turned. It was him. He spun around and ran to the corner. He disappeared.

Oriana walked along the cars the boys had hid behind, sucking frigid air into her taxed lungs as she looked, illogically and irrationally, for his reappearance. She wasn't sure if the ache in her chest was from her sprint through the school or from the devastation of what she just witnessed. She leaned back against a car and bent over, breathing hard.

Dez wasn't just a user. He was a dealer. She feared her heart might break.

Chapter Seven

*"Send out your light and your truth;
let them lead me."*
– Psalm 43:3a

The cell phone vibrated only once against the countertop, signaling a voicemail message.

Nicanor picked up his jacket and went to the phone. One missed call, the screen told him, as if that were news. He looked at the number listed. Terry again. Hard to believe how much the agent used to fawn over Nicanor when his career was going well. Getting into trouble and refusing jobs was apparently the fast track to getting on Terry's bad side. His latest calls had been getting nastier. He seemed to finally be getting the idea that Nicanor really meant to leave his career, and a whole new Terry was emerging. Instead of being Terry's treasured star, Nicanor felt more like a sponge Terry was determined to squeeze blood from, until the last drop.

"Nicanor, you need to call me." Terry's sharp voice in the message made Nicanor hold the phone away from his ear as he listened. "If you're really done, you owe me some serious back payments. I suggest you dance them off. I need to know where you are. Give me your address or get back here before I get lawyers involved. I don't want this to get ugly. And I won't be able to get you any gigs unless you come back pronto. This is ridiculous. Call me."

If Terry hadn't turned out to be such a loan shark, Nicanor might feel bad for his ex-agent. In the last three years, Terry lost three of the top tango dancers in the country. And each one because of what Nicanor had done. Terry probably knew that, but he was greedy enough not to let it show as long as Nicanor was still making money for him. Money was the only reason Terry still cared Nicanor was alive now, but there was no point in his frequent calls.

Nicanor barely had enough for this apartment, even skipping most meals. And he was not ready to go back. He couldn't go back. He had his fill of trying to work in New York while pretending he was guiltless and free, taking advantage of the hole in the tango world left by Dante. The life in New York was an empty sham, and Nicanor didn't deserve even that kind of existence.

He didn't know how much longer he would last, how much longer he should be allowed to continue living without paying a greater price. At least here he was helping Nye a little. He was helping her sister. Perhaps if he could protect Oriana from the dangers she was so unprepared for with her naïve optimism, it would be like saving a life to pay for the one he had destroyed.

Did the universe work like that? He hoped so. There was no other reason to put on his jacket, leave the apartment, and take the bus to the school. There was no other reason not to end the pain in his soul right now.

"No. You." Nicanor pointed to the dark-haired boy he thought was called Antonio. "Three steps, not four. Listen to the music."

Tiny Maria watched him with rounded eyes as she naturally did the steps correctly, apparently without needing to concentrate.

He gave her a small, close-lipped smile. He wasn't used to making that expression, but the try was worth it to get a shy smile in return before she dropped her gaze. He had never seen anyone quite so pretty and innocently endearing as the little girl.

Except, perhaps, for her teacher.

He looked to see Oriana stand up from the chair she had sat on only a minute. She was like a nervous butterfly today—not sure where she was going or how to act. One moment, she was affectionate and beaming at the children as usual, gracing Nicanor with a few of her bright smiles. The next moment, she watched the class with the look of one who saw nothing as she chewed on her lower lip or held her fingers to her mouth, like the remnants of an old nail-biting habit.

As if she just came back from a thousand miles away, Oriana saw Nicanor watching her. She smiled, but it looked forced. She turned her gaze to the children, then checked her watch. She looked at Nicanor and mouthed, "It's time."

He went to the old portable CD player Oriana had provided and turned off the music. "That's all for today," he said to the children, though he didn't look at them. "Practice at home."

"Kids, let's thank Mr. Pessoa for the great class today." Oriana stepped among the group of children as some of them recited the mandatory thank you. "Don't forget, pictures for tomorrow—anything that shows something special or that makes you happy. And don't forget to pick up your stuff from the classroom on your way out," she added, raising her voice to be heard by the children who had already escaped into the hallway.

She turned and cast her smile on Nicanor, but it fell short of her usual sparkling standards.

"The boy was not here today."

She blinked at him. Then she nodded. "Dez. I saw him yesterday. He was …" She glanced at the empty doorway before continuing. "He was selling drugs to another boy."

Her brown eyes held something he had never seen there—sadness. They welled with moisture, and a tear started to stream down her cheek. She swiped it away with the back of her hand. "Sorry." She managed a watery half-smile. "I've always been the emotional sister."

Something in his chest stirred at the depth of love she must have for these children, even the streetwise boy on drugs. "No apologies."

"Right." She sniffed.

"You care very much. Why?" He couldn't fathom such compassion for kids who were not her own—street children with only attitude and hate in their hearts.

Unshed tears glistened in the eyes she turned toward him. "These kids are getting killed before they have a chance to live. The streets, the drugs, gangs. Somebody has to fight for them." She glanced away, then met his gaze again, another tear tracking down her cheek. "I have to believe I can save them."

Nicanor stared at her. Would things have turned out differently if someone had fought to save him?

She wiped the remaining moisture from her face and eyes, as if wiping away her sadness. It must have worked, because the light came back into those eyes and she brightened, magically back to her usual spirits.

Nothing seemed able to keep her down long. Where did she find her endless source of happiness?

"Anyway, thanks for teaching the class. I think it went well for the first time. What did you think? Did you like the kids? I hope they weren't too much trouble."

Just like that, she was back to the flurry of questions. He

thought a moment to pick the question to answer. "They're rough, but a few have potential."

"Nye said she thought LaTisha had a head start from being into hip-hop already."

"The movement is different. She moves by force, not grace. She must start over for ballroom and tango. Maria will be better."

"Maria? Nye could barely get her to move at all. She's so shy. I confess I wasn't paying as much attention today as I should have."

"She is natural."

"I'm glad. She needs something to build her confidence." Oriana went over to the CD player where it sat on a chair and unplugged it from the wall. "Maybe dance could do that."

"Why is she here?"

She straightened, winding up the cord. "Ah, you mean, what's a sweet little thing like that doing with the 'at-risk' kids?" She made quotation marks with the fingers of her free hand. "Yeah, she doesn't really belong in my class. Her grades dropped really far last year because she has dyslexia. We don't have much of a special ed. program here, so she gets the 'troubled' label and ends up with a group of kids she's scared to death of."

She bunched the folded cord in her hand and lifted the CD player by the handle. "That unfortunately happens from time to time. LaTisha's another one who doesn't deserve the placement or the reputation. She's just made some bad choices in who her friends are, but she's staying pretty clean herself so far. She really wants to do the right thing and has such a caring heart."

LaTisha wasn't the only one. Oriana's love for the girls was obvious in her earnest tone and soft smile.

"You take care of them."

She looked at him, giving him that special smile. "I try." She swung the CD player at her side as she walked to the chair by the door where she had left her purse.

He followed at a distance.

"I think it's easier for the girls to trust me sooner than the boys." She picked up her purse and turned back to him. "It will be good for them to have you as their teacher. They need male role models."

He stopped walking, his throat tightening. He couldn't possibly be a role model. "I'm only a dance instructor," he said firmly, hoping she would get the message if she had really meant what she said.

"A teacher is always a role model. The kids will be watching you. Especially the boys."

"Then tell them not to." He didn't try to hide the sharpness of the words. "I teach dance only."

She blinked at him. "Okay. I'm sorry."

He couldn't miss the hurt in her eyes as she turned away. He swallowed. "What will you do?"

She looked back. "Do?"

"About the boy."

"I'll have to report what I know to the police and Harry, the principal." She checked her watch. "Actually, I better get going and do that now." The moment of pain had already passed and the sparkle was back in her eyes. "Do you need a lift?"

The offer was tempting, but he knew she was just being kind. "No."

"Okay. Oh, I almost forgot. With next Thursday being Thanksgiving, I wondered if you'd be able to do the class earlier in the week instead. Maybe Tuesday or Wednesday?"

"I'll have to check."

"Oh, that's right—you're teaching other classes at the studio now. Well, just let me know. Can you lock up when you leave?"

"Yes."

"Thanks again."

He savored her smile in his mind's eye long after she had vanished into the dark hallway.

Oriana sat on the hard bench that lined the wall and watched uniformed police officers pass by.

"So that's why you're at the police station." Nye's voice through the phone was like a soothing balm in this foreign atmosphere. The fact that Oriana hadn't ended up at the police station before this was really a miracle, considering the students she had been teaching for three years.

"Yeah."

"Well, I'm glad we got that cleared up. Mother would have had a fit if she had been the one to call and you told her you were there."

"No kidding." Oriana felt as wide-eyed as LaTisha as she watched an officer escort a big, bearded tough in handcuffs past the bench.

"I'm sorry, Oriana. It must be hard to have to do that. I know you had a lot of hope for Dez."

"I still do." Oriana needed the reminder herself. "Maybe this will be what Dez needs. You know, the jolt that gets him to see what happens when you mess around with this kind of stuff."

"You don't think they'll send him to jail, do you?"

"Oh, my." Oriana sucked in a breath. "I hope not." She hadn't really considered that. She just knew she had to report that she had seen a drug sale. It wouldn't be right to do anything else. But the thought of Dez, still just a little boy, behind bars or the mesh fence of a yard at a juvenile detention facility sent shivers down her spine.

An elderly woman with a cane, her salt and pepper hair pulled into a bun at the nape of her neck, shuffled over to the bench and sat on the other end.

"Did he show up at class today?" Nye asked.

"No."

"Too bad. I was curious how he would get along with Nicanor."

"Yeah." Oriana laughed, earning a suspicious look from the woman on the bench. "The kids were a little shocked, I think. He's definitely more of a task master than you are."

"I was hoping he would go easier on them, since they're so young. I don't think he's ever taught children, though."

"Honestly, I think his approach was good for them. They can be a handful for anyone who lacks authority."

"That's definitely not a problem for Nicanor."

"Ah, no." Oriana chuckled. She had been a tad worried about how the kids would respond to Nic, but his muscular physique and the intensity that so obviously smoldered just beneath that implacable exterior seemed to give him an instant street cred with the boys, even Juan. Still, it wouldn't hurt if Nic were a little more of a friendly mentor. "Does Nic ever smile?"

"Nic?"

Oriana grinned guiltily, though her sister couldn't see it. "Yeah. 'Nicanor' is so serious and formal."

"Do you call him that to his face?" Disbelief saturated Nye's voice.

"No, not yet. I think it fits him, don't you?"

"No comment."

"Okay." Oriana rolled her eyes. "Well, can you at least

answer my question? Does he smile? I haven't seen one since the accident. Even before then, Dante was the only one who could get him to."

"Hmm. Maybe I'll have to make that my mission—to make him smile." Oriana tried to imagine what that dark, brooding face would look like with the mouth upturned and teeth showing. She bet he had an awesome smile.

"I think they call that mission: impossible, but you're the one to do it."

"Thank you. I think."

"Speaking of Nicanor, I was wondering if you'd mind if I invited him for Thanksgiving."

There was that flutter in her stomach again. "No, of course not. Why would I mind?"

"I didn't really think you would. I just wanted to warn you."

"I see. Avoiding a repeat of Mom's surprise invite of Cullen to their anniversary last year?"

"Right."

"Well, thank you. But, as I said, Nic and I are not involved."

"Isn't 'just friends' the normal phrase?"

Heat flushed Oriana's face. She was glad the lady who threw her crazy-person glances now and then was the only one there to see the blush. "I thought it might be a little too early to assume that."

"Wow, you are being careful."

Oriana could hear the grin in Nye's voice. She tried to change the subject. "Have you ever asked Nic to church?"

Nye was silent a moment. "No, I guess not. To tell you the truth, I never even thought of it. Dante used to try to get him to go, but he never would. Something to do with his mother or his father, I think. I don't know that he'd want to be asked now either. I'm positive he wouldn't go. He won't even come to dinner at my house, though I keep asking."

"Well, maybe he'd come to small group if I asked him." She was fishing, and she knew it. Hopefully, Nye would be as tactful as usual and not comment on Oriana's obvious desperation. The churning in her stomach was enough to warn her she was headed in a bad direction if she was hoping to convert Nic so she could safely fall in love with him.

"Maybe. I guess there shouldn't be any harm in asking. It would be great if you could get him to go, but … just don't get your hopes up too high."

"Of course." Oriana tried to interject her voice with indifference. "You know I invite everyone I see to church."

"Right. And Nicanor is just like anybody else to you."

How did they end up back here again? "Yes, he is." She hoped her automatic response was true.

"Well, since I know you feel that way, I can tell you the real reason I called."

Oriana sighed inwardly at getting let off the interrogation hook. "Which is?"

"As I said, Nicanor won't come to dinner when I ask him, but I feel terrible about him sitting alone in his apartment all the time. I don't think it's good for him right now."

She'd get no argument from Oriana on that score. The man was definitely fighting some demons, or depression, at the very least.

"So I'm very happy that I've convinced him to go to a dance concert with us tomorrow night."

"How in the world did you manage that?" The idea of Nic going out and having fun at a show of any sort was hard to imagine.

"Long story, but suffice it to say I told him I'm considering having our students do one of the dances for a recital, and I wanted his opinion."

"You mean you twisted his arm."

"Basically, yes."

Oriana chuckled. "Well, congrats, even if you had to be conniving."

"Thanks, I think, but I really wanted to ask you if you'd come, too."

Oriana almost dropped the phone. "What?" she managed to rasp out.

"I'm afraid it will be too awkward for Nicanor with just Cullen and me. He might feel like the third wheel and all that."

"So you want to double."

"No!" Nye exclaimed, startling Oriana. "*Not* like a date."

Oriana had to smile at Nye's extreme reaction.

"I wouldn't have asked you if I thought it might be taken that way, but I'm sure Nicanor won't think of it like that."

Oriana couldn't help but wonder, with a little spark of irritation, why Nye was so sure Nicanor couldn't be interested in her sister. Maybe because he had never liked Nye, who was obviously the more beautiful one. As soon as the thought came into her mind, Oriana wanted to kick it out. The green-eyed monster was getting way too comfortable in her head lately.

"You told me *you* don't feel that way," Nye continued, seemingly unaware of Oriana's internal struggle. "Right?"

Oriana opened her mouth to answer but wasn't sure what to say. Had she said that exactly? Was it true?

Oriana looked up and sighed with relief. The conversation was about to be interrupted by an officer who headed from the staircase to where she sat. He was at least four inches taller than Nye's 6'3" husband, and his muscular, linebacker build made him an intimidating figure in the uniform. Oriana had never been so glad she was not a criminal. "Gotta go, Nye."

"Sure you do."

"For real."

"Oh, no." Nye groaned. "You're starting to talk like your students again."

"Very funny. Talk later."

"Wait—are you coming tomorrow night?"

"Sure, yes, okay. Bye." Oriana ended the call, trying not to think about what she had just committed to as the giant officer stopped in front of her. She stood, nerves tingling as she remembered what she was about to do. "Officer Kelly?"

A warm smile contrasted with his dark skin as he extended a massive hand. "Call me Gabe." The words came out in a low-pitched rumble.

Her breathing started to calm with his unexpected friendliness. She swallowed as she plunged her hand into his. "I have to report a drug dealer."

She had done scarier things. Oriana had once found her way back to the cabins at youth camp in the dark, alone after a game of capture the flag gone wrong. The shadows among the black bushes and trees could have held bears, mountain lions, wolves, or even snakes. To the mind of an eight-year-old girl who was terrified of the dark, that night of nearly getting lost and needing to find her way to safety was life-shaping. The experience ended up being a good one, since Oriana came to trust Jesus as her Savior because of it. But it still went down on record as the most terrifying moment of her life.

That is, until tonight. Oriana looked at herself in the tall mirror of the ladies' restroom one more time, smoothing the front of her black dress with her hand. This was not a date. Not a date.

She forced out a long, calming breath, trying to prepare to leave the restroom. Of course it wasn't a date. Nye and Cullen had picked her up and Nic met them at the theater. Hardly a date scenario.

She had to get back to reality. It didn't help that she and Nic sat next to each other during the performance. She felt guilty that Nye and Cullen paid for her ticket, since she didn't notice a bit of the dancing with Nic so close. She had all she could do to stop watching him out of the corner of her eye.

Now the concert was over, and he had only looked at her about three times and talked even less. Oriana gladly grabbed at the excuse to follow Nye to the restroom when it presented itself. Maybe a good look in the mirror would tell her why Nic was so easily able to ignore her. Oriana turned sideways and narrowed her eyes at her reflection. Was that a bulge at her waistline?

"You look beautiful," Nye said, suddenly at Oriana's side.

How had Oriana not seen her approach in the mirror? Nye was more stunning than ever in the shimmering blue gown that made her blue eyes pop and her blonde hair shine. Looking from this epitome of model-like beauty and elegance to her own reflection made Oriana feel like the ugliest warthog in the room. She swallowed. "So do you."

"You looked like you were far away."

"Just lost in thought, I guess."

"Thinking about Dez?"

A pang of real guilt hit Oriana's conscience. She hadn't thought of him once tonight.

"Or maybe a different guy?"

Oriana looked at Nye in feigned shock. "You're impossible. If you don't stop, you're going to get me falling for him, which I didn't think you wanted me to do." She wrinkled her nose at her sister's reflection and headed for the door out of the restroom. She paused and looked back. "Are you coming?"

"Yes." Nye didn't bother to hide her amused smile.

Oriana knew she couldn't blame Nye for the little cartwheel her heart performed when she saw Nic standing with Cullen in the lobby. Nic had shown up in his usual black T-shirt and jeans with the black jacket, but the informal outfit didn't keep him from drawing many second looks from women as they walked by. He and Cullen made quite a pair.

"Sorry we took so long," Nye apologized, as they reached the men and she took Cullen's offered arm.

"You're worth the wait." Pure adoration shone from the gaze Cullen turned on his wife.

Oriana stifled the urge to roll her eyes, even as his obvious love threatened to call out the green-eyed monster. He had been more lovey-dovey than usual ever since they found out about the baby. The coddling was sweet but slightly nauseating.

Oriana sighed. What was wrong with her? Up until lately she had felt so content and happy with her single life.

"Are you all right?"

Oriana turned toward the quiet voice and found herself staring into the blue eyes of the real reason for her sudden discontentment.

For the first time that evening, Nic met her gaze, his eyes holding concern.

Little butterflies took to flight in her stomach. "Yes, I'm fine. Thank you." Her mouth stretched into what was probably a silly schoolgirl smile.

"So." Cullen looked at them, apparently done fawning over Nye for the moment. "Mario's for dinner?"

"Sure." Oriana shrugged a shoulder.

"I must go," Nic announced out of the blue.

"Are you sure?" Nye's brow furrowed. "We'd love to have you join us. We can pick a different restaurant, if you like."

"No. Thank you." He looked only at Nye. "I'll talk to you about the dance on Monday."

Nye nodded. "Okay. Can we drop you at your place?"

He just met her gaze for a moment, and they seemed to communicate in that silent language of theirs.

Nye smiled gently. "Thank you for coming. I'll see you on Monday."

This Shadow

A brusque nod was Nic's response before he started to go without a good-bye to anyone else.

"Nicanor?" Oriana blurted before she thought, at least remembering not to use her nickname for him.

He turned as she took a few steps to catch up to him.

She had no idea what she was going to say, but lack of words was never her problem. "I wanted to ask you something," she started in a nervous rush. "Would you be interested in going to my small group sometime? I know you're new to the city, and it can be hard to meet people. Some of my best friends are in the group."

He raised an eyebrow. "Small group?"

"Oh, sorry." Heat rushed to her face. "It's some people from my church. Just seven of us. We get together at my apartment for Bible study and to hang out. We play games sometimes, eat good food. It's a fun time."

He watched her for a moment. "I don't think so," he finally answered.

"Oh, okay." She tried to hide her disappointment behind a smile. Nye had warned her. "Well, let me know if you ever change your mind. We meet Tuesday nights. It used to be Fridays, but now … it's changed … so …" She trailed off in humiliation. Why could she never stop talking?

He gave her that short nod and turned away, not meeting her eyes.

Oriana sighed again as she watched him leave.

"Didn't work?" Nye stopped next to Oriana.

"What?"

"Getting him to smile."

Oriana snorted in response. "I think getting him to be able to stand looking at me for more than a second might be a prerequisite. Doesn't do much for a girl's self-esteem to be treated like she has the plague or something."

"I thought he was just like anyone else to you. 'Just friends' and all that."

Oriana gave Nye a stare. "Maybe 'friends' was an overstatement."

Nye smiled sympathetically and put her arm around Oriana's shoulders. "Don't worry. I haven't met anyone yet who could resist my little sister's charm or God's love. You'll get through."

Oriana returned Nye's smile, her heart lifting with the hope that her big sister was right.

Chapter Eight

*"I form light and create darkness,
I make well-being and create calamity,
I am the Lord, who does all these things."*
– Isaiah 45:7

Six days. Oriana made herself continue up the stairs to the third floor of the school, her tired legs dragging. That's what she got for pacing around her apartment all night. She thought telling the police about Dez would be the hard part, but the waiting was really wearing her down. Almost a week had passed since she went to the station, and the police still hadn't seen or heard any more of Dez than she had, though they said they would start watching him and his brother.

She couldn't stop thinking about her lost student, wondering where he was and if he was safe. Did he know she had reported him? He knew she had seen him, at least, and that was enough to make him stay away from school.

She blew out a puff of air. So much for helping Dez pick up his grades. Even as the thought passed through her mind, the ache in her chest recognized that grades were the least of her worries now.

"You okay, Miss Sanders?"

Oriana looked up to see LaTisha waiting for her on the landing like she used to, but this time at the beginning of the third flight of stairs. Oriana put on a smile. "Yes. Just thinking."

"So we get dance class today?" LaTisha's shifted her weight back and forth, as if she couldn't hold still if her life depended on it.

Oriana had to stifle a chuckle at the girl's excitement. "Yes, dance class is today. And hello."

"Hi." LaTisha giggled, something Oriana had never heard her do, and jumped up the stairs ahead of her teacher.

Oriana followed the bouncing girl, her own spirits lifting for some inexplicable reason. Probably just because having the dance class a day early reminded her that Thanksgiving was tomorrow. But Thanksgiving had never made her heart skip a beat like the thought of the man who might be waiting in the dance room.

LaTisha spun around at the top of the stairs. "He's cute, don't you think?" she whispered dramatically behind the hand she held next to her mouth.

Oriana's cheeks warmed. Thinking along the same lines as a sixth-grader was probably not a good sign. Thankfully, a response wasn't required since LaTisha skipped off down the hall toward the light from the dance room.

Oriana shook her head as she headed the same direction. Maybe they just shared a natural female reaction. A full four days had dragged by since she had last seen Nic, after all, and there hadn't been much in the way of pleasant things besides him to think about during that time.

Oriana's worry, mixed with periodic twinges of guilt, was enough to take a toll on her usual energy level. She tried not to let anything show when teaching her other kids, but the extra empty chair and even the new dominance Juan enjoyed in Dez's absence were reminders of the student she feared she had lost.

She should leave the whole thing in God's hands, and she did that every morning during her quiet time and Bible study. By the time she arrived at school, she had grabbed it back from Him again and was trying to carry the burden herself.

"Lord," she quietly prayed, as she stopped just outside the door to the dance room, "please give me your peace about Dez. Watch over him, protect him, and please show me how to help him. Show me what to do, Lord. Enable me to be what he needs right now." She opened her eyes and took a deep breath, renewed energy coursing through her veins. Remembering her goal to make Nic smile, she entered the dance room armed with a big one herself. Nothing could rattle her now.

Her heart took a flying leap that contradicted her bravado when she saw Nic, already directing LaTisha, Antonio, Maria, and Brayden into position. Another black T-shirt set off Nic's contoured biceps and dark toned skin in a way that left her in no doubt as to why Nye's adult evening classes, with Nic as instructor, were filling up with so many women. Heaven help her. She should have prayed about Nic and her heart condition.

She did just that a half-hour into the class when Nic suddenly looked at her and flicked his fingers to indicate she should come over. "Me?" A stupid question, since the only other people in the room were the kids clustered around him.

"You must demonstrate."

She walked over as slowly as she could, her heart pounding in her ears. "Umm, Nye's the dancer in our family. I never did that. Unless you count three months of ballet lessons when I was six."

Nic didn't look like he was paying any attention to her excuses.

She stopped a couple feet away from him. "I was terrible."

"I'll help you. Come." He directed her closer.

He wanted them to dance together? She was sure from the heat that her face turned beet red.

"Go on, Miss Sanders," LaTisha encouraged.

Oriana glanced at the impressionable faces of her students, all watching her. Trying to act like an adult, Oriana stepped close to Nic. Too close. She moistened her dry lips. "What are we demonstrating?"

He put one hand on her back and took her dangling hand in his other one. "Partnering with the waltz."

"The waltz. Okay." Nye had made her do the waltz a couple times when they were kids and Nye wanted to practice.

Oriana always stepped on her sister's feet until Nye gave up in frustration. Oriana knew she wouldn't be any better now when all she could think about was the warm press of Nic's hand at her back, her hand in his, and how close his face was to hers.

He seemed to have no such difficulty concentrating. His expression was as intense as ever when he met her gaze with his, those electric blue eyes like a jolt at this proximity. "Follow me."

His leg moved forward, and she looked down to pull her foot back.

"No." He pressed the hand at her back more firmly against her. "Look at me."

That would be easier to do if she could remember to breathe with his face so close to hers. Maybe the eye-contact avoidance he was usually so fond of would work. She stared at his left temple, where she noticed a small scar she had never seen before. The faint, pale-colored line started just above his eyebrow and traveled at an angle upward, where it disappeared into his black hair.

"Right on, Miss Sanders." Antonio's young voice betrayed a good dose of amusement in his compliment.

Oriana suddenly became aware that, while she was engaged in her study of Nic's face, she had been responding naturally to his movements. He *must* be a good dancer if he could make one out of her so quickly. It felt as natural as walking to follow the touch of his hand and shift in the directions he communicated through his graceful movements. She looked at her feet to see how they were doing steps she didn't know and stepped squarely on his shoe.

"Oh, I'm so sorry." She pulled away, her face on fire.

"You're fine." His words were kind, but he avoided her gaze and looked more irritated than usual.

Boy, now she'd really done it. She had warned him she was clumsy.

He turned to the children. "You see, the man leads, and the girl can follow, but only if you lead well. Pair up again and try it. Very slowly." He pressed a button on the CD player to restart the music track, as Oriana slunk back to her chair. She wished she could disappear behind the wall, taking her mortification and confusion with her. Why had he asked her to demo if he was going to get mad when she messed up?

She lifted her heavy hair off her neck and held it up briefly to cool her neck. She watched the class resume, with Nic acting as if nothing had happened. Well, that was something to be thankful for, she supposed. Clearly, the inappropriate feelings she was having were one-sided.

Nicanor didn't know why he had thought dancing with Oriana would be a good idea. He hadn't thought of anything but needing to demonstrate to the students until she looked at him with huge eyes. She reminded him of a rabbit he had once seen on the path at Central Park. The little animal had stared at him like that just before it took off as fast as it could. Oriana looked as cute and appealing as the rabbit when she slowly made her way over to him, and she was just as innocent of her effect.

There was no backing out at that point, even when he discovered the danger of holding her close, in his arms. He had danced with countless women in his career, at parties, on dates, but he had never had this kind of reaction before. He had been attracted to several, of course. Their business was to be beautiful, and they were. Yet he had never met anyone like Oriana. Being so near to her, seeing her nervousness and her blush, softened and warmed something inside him. He feared she had sparked a small flame of feeling—a flicker that could turn into a fire if he wasn't careful.

He was glad she had stepped on his foot and stopped the dance. She was Nye's sister. Any idea of a future was impossible. If Nye found out the truth someday, or if she never did and Nicanor carried it with him forever, his guilt would destroy him and anything he had with Oriana. Even she would never smile at him again if she knew the kind of man he really was. She was so happy and innocent. She should be protected from men like him. He would never deserve anyone like her.

"Class, say thanks to Mr. Pessoa." Oriana's closing remark brought Nicanor back to the present as the students again said their programmed thank yous and trotted away. All but Maria, who hung back and looked up at Nicanor.

"Happy Thanksgiving, Mr. Pessoa," she whispered, with the tiniest of smiles.

"Happy Thanksgiving, Maria." A different kind of warmth touched his heart. Perhaps he was developing a weakness for brown-eyed females.

Her shy smile widened as she ducked away and ran out of the room.

"Well, I like that. Not even a good-bye to me." Oriana's sparkling grin belied her words. "I hear you're joining us for Thanksgiving dinner tomorrow."

"Nye asked." He didn't add that he wasn't going to go.

"Does that mean you aren't coming?"

He gave her a quick glance, surprised she had noticed his avoidance. "No."

"So you're coming."

"No," he repeated, irritated by her misunderstanding of her question.

"Why not? Are you spending it with family somewhere? You aren't going back to New York, are you?"

"No."

She smiled, her eyes glinting with humor. "You've got the trick of it."

He raised an eyebrow.

"My dad does it that way. He just answers the last question and leaves the rest."

Not knowing what he should say to being positively compared to her father, he busied himself with unplugging the CD player.

"Do you want to just hang on to that yourself? I don't really use it right now."

He hesitated.

"Oh, I didn't think," she answered for him. "It'd be awkward to take it home on the bus, wouldn't it? I feel bad about you taking the bus all the time. Are you sure I can't drop you off at home?"

"Yes," he hurried to say. After today, he knew they should see each other as little as possible.

"Okay." She went over to the CD player, ending up less than a foot away from him.

Nicanor watched her as she picked it up, much more aware of her closeness than he had been before. He could smell her perfume, or perhaps the fresh scent was from her hair. Why had he danced with her? Add that to his endless list of mistakes.

"I really hope you'll come for dinner tomorrow. Nobody should spend Thanksgiving alone."

There. He was a charity case to her, nothing more. Good. He picked up his jacket from the back of the chair the CD player had sat on.

"We'd really like to have you there, Nic."

He started at the nickname and looked at her. *Nicky.* His mother's voice echoed in his mind. There was always so much love in the way she said the word.

Oriana held her hand over her mouth. "I—I'm sorry. Is it okay if I call you Nic?"

He thought for a moment, not sure himself. She looked so worried, those brown eyes watching him anxiously as she bit her lip. It wasn't such a big thing to make her happy. He shifted his jacket to hang by a finger off his shoulder. "If you wish." He took a last, passing look at the smile that lit her face as he headed for the door.

Oriana breathed heavily as she slowed from a sprint near her apartment building. She walked toward the path that led to the building entrance, resting her hands on her hips. It felt good to turn onto the bush-lined path and get out of the wind. The night was awfully nippy for a run.

Her fingers were freezing, but her hair was still wet with sweat under the hat she pulled off as she walked toward the door. Her phone vibrated in her jacket pocket. She stopped her mp3 player and pulled the ear buds out of her ears as she unzipped her pocket and grabbed the phone. Her running gloves were foolishly thin for this weather, but at least she could handle her phone with them on.

"Hello?" She twisted the speaker away, trying to hide her panting.

"Miss Sanders?"

"Dez? Is that you?" Oriana couldn't keep the excitement and concern from her voice.

"Yeah. Can you come to school?" He sounded strange, worried. Maybe scared.

"What is it, Dez? Are you in trouble?" Dumb question, considering she had just reported him for drug dealing.

"I ... I need your help."

"I want to help you, Dez. Maybe we can talk about what's been happening. You don't have to hide from me or the police. We all want to help you."

"Can you come to school?"

"When?"

"At midnight."

"Tonight?"

"Yeah."

The abandoned school, downtown, in the middle of the night? That did not sound good. Oriana went to the door, fumbling for the keys in her pocket with numb fingers. "Why don't I come and pick you up from wherever you are now? We could just talk. You wouldn't have to tell me anything you didn't want to."

There was a long pause on Dez's end while Oriana opened the door and went thankfully into the warmth of the dim hallway. She thought she could hear another voice in the background.

"We can talk at school. You gotta come alone. Please." A note of fear definitely laced his voice this time. "I'll have to run away again if you don't come."

Oriana looked at her watch. *8:15*. She sighed, far from comfortable with the idea, but she would never forgive herself if she didn't go when Dez was obviously scared and finally asking her for help. He was turning to her when in trouble. The least she could do was return the trust. "Okay, I'll be there."

"Meet me outside at the back." He paused. "By the gym."

The poor boy was so intent on hiding. "I know you're scared, Dez, but it's going to be okay."

Silence.

"Dez?"

She looked at her phone. Call ended. He must have hung up.

Oriana's mind raced as she walked to her apartment and went inside. What kind of trouble was Dez in now, and why was he calling her? He had never shown this kind of trust in her before, but she had felt they were developing a bond, that maybe he was starting to see her as different from the other authority figures he resented so much.

She wanted to prove that she was different, that he could count on her when he was in trouble. She had been afraid he would see her as the enemy who ratted him out to the police.

He must not, since he called her for help. Going to that area at midnight might not be entirely safe, but she had to go alone, or Dez would bolt. If she went alone like he asked, she'd show he could trust her, and she would have a much better shot at talking him into going with her to the police.

Oriana went through the motions of taking off her running shoes and peeling off her damp jacket as she thought through her game plan. She didn't have to be completely stupid, which she had to admit going alone probably would be. She could take someone along in the car, and then get out by herself to see Dez. At least she'd have backup if something went wrong. But who could she call? Nye wouldn't want to go, so she would probably try to talk Oriana out of going herself and might succeed. She was out. Their mother—world champion worrier—was a definite no.

Oriana went to her bedroom and grabbed some warm clothes, her sweaty pullover causing a chill that made her hurry to get to the shower. She could call her dad. He was understanding and even-keeled, but he would probably have to tell her mother where he was going, which would result in the avalanche of motherly concern Oriana hoped to avoid.

Oriana went to the bathroom and turned on the lights. The vibrant colors of the room, the red and blue Nye said looked too patriotic, did their usual job of calming her and banishing negativity. It really wasn't that big of a deal. She was only meeting a twelve-year-old boy, and by the school—not exactly a popular nighttime hangout for gangs. Maybe she could go alone.

Nic. She froze with her hand on the faucet when the idea hit her. She would call Nic. She had gotten his cell number in case of cancellations or problems at school, but she had never used it. He was impartial enough that she was sure he wouldn't try to dissuade her, and they certainly weren't close enough for him to worry too much.

Ignoring the little twinge of regret which accompanied that thought, she started the water for the shower. She could still see the shocked expression on his face when she had accidentally called him Nic. She wouldn't be surprised if he didn't want to go with her after that. Regardless, at least she would have told someone what she was doing. That should make her mother happy.

***

Oriana sat in the darkness of the car and pressed the backlight button on her watch as she held the cell phone to her ear. Five minutes before midnight.

"You have reached six ..."

Oriana sighed as the computerized voicemail recording came on again. She lowered the phone and ended the call. So much for not going alone. She had tried calling Nic three times during the last few hours, but only reached his voicemail. At least she hoped it was his. There was no name recorded, so she could have his number wrong. Good thing she had only left one message.

Her final attempt to call him was pointless, since he could never get there on time. She probably only gave it a shot because looking out into the darkness behind the school was making her nervous. The back of the building faced a little-used street that didn't have street lights—a fact she hadn't been aware of since she never went there at night. She didn't think of herself as a fearful person, but this situation was a little out of the ordinary. The situation was so different from how safe and relaxed she had felt when Nic had gone with her to see Dez's mother.

Oriana blew out a forceful breath. Such thoughts were what made her try his number one last time, and they weren't doing her courage, or lack of it, any good. She had God with her, and that was all the protection she needed. "Dear Lord," she prayed quietly, "please keep me safe, and enable me to help Dez. Please soften his heart toward You and bring him to You through all this trouble. Let your light shine through me tonight, Father, so that Dez may see it and want your light in his own life. Amen."

A sense of peace flowed through her, replacing her fears with an impenetrable calm. She was ready.

She double checked that her car door actually locked before she started across the street. At least the moon provided enough light to walk by. She reached the other side of the street and stopped, scanning the sidewalk in one direction, then the other. Everything was so quiet. So dark.

Where was Dez? She lit up her watch again. *12:01*. He could just be late. Or maybe he meant they were supposed to meet right by the door to the gym, which was set back from the sidewalk through a gate a little farther down from where she was.

She headed slowly in that direction, looking around cautiously as she went. So much for her faith—her nervousness was already coming back. She reached the gate, which was open as usual. There was only darkness beyond it. "Dez?" She said the word quietly, but it broke the silence like the blare of a horn.

Nothing.

She started to turn away from the gate.

"Miss Sanders," a boy whispered.

She turned back. "Dez? Is that you?" She squinted into the darkness by the building, but couldn't make out anything other than two large garbage bins.

"In here." The voice sounded like Dez.

Not knowing why she felt so scared, she cautiously stepped just inside the gate. She was being ridiculous. He was just a little kid. Tired of her own childishness, she lifted her shoulders and stalked farther inside, headed for where she thought the gym door was.

"You sure look scared, teacher lady."

Oriana jumped at the man's voice as the accompanying body emerged from the darkness next to one of the trash bins. His dark skin made his face difficult to read in the shadows, but she saw enough in his flashing eyes to know the sneer wasn't friendly.

She froze, not sure what to do.

"Wondering who I am, right?"

She didn't respond, far too busy trying to spot the door to the gym without looking like she was searching for it. She had her keys with her—she could maybe get in if she got a head start.

He sauntered toward her at a casual, slow pace. "You squealed on my little brother."

"You're James?"

"You know my name." He put a hand to his chest in mock gratefulness. "I'm touched."

She watched him as he got closer. "Where's Dez?"

"You trippin'. What kind of teacher flips her student to the cops and then acts like she cares?"

Righteous anger churned in her stomach, giving her the courage to look James straight in the eyes. "What kind of man turns his brother into a pusher?"

He stopped a few feet away and stared at her. "Either you got a lot of spunk, or you're just stupid, teacher lady."

"Maybe I am stupid, since I thought Dez would be here."

"Oh, he's here."

"I don't see him."

He gave her a rapper-style point and lifted his chin, a nasty scowl replacing the sneer. "You don't see a lot of things." He lowered his hand. "Come on out, boys."

Four men, two of them more like sixteen-year-old boys, came out from the darkness by the building and near the garbage bins.

She tried to swallow, but her mouth and throat were too dry. *Lord, help me.* "What do you want, James?" she finally managed.

"You a teacher, right? We gonna do the teaching tonight. Gonna teach you a little lesson on not finking to the cops."

"Don't do anything stupid, James." She held up a shaking hand and glanced over her shoulder to the gate, now about ten feet away.

"Oh, now she calling me stupid," he said loudly, for the benefit of his buddies. "That ain't nice, teacher lady."

She made a move to run, but his hand grabbed her arm. He yanked her back and jerked her against him as he pulled her toward the darkness by the wall of the building. "And here little bro says you like to talk about God and Jesus all the time," he muttered in her ear, as she tried to twist away from his hot breath. "Well, just turn the other cheek, right?" He chuckled, a nasty sound.

"Please, just let me go. I only came here to help Dez. You have to believe me." She could see the other thugs coming up behind James. She tried not to think of what they were planning to do. Her mind clambered for a way to fight him off. His grip was like a vice on her arm.

James twisted her around so that her back was against him, his arm wrapped tightly around her neck. The leather of his sleeve was a cold shock on her skin, but she was soon more worried about breathing. Maybe an elbow thrust into his chest, if she could just—

She saw what James wanted her to.

Dez stood partially in the shadow of the wall, but she recognized his small, thin form. He was watching.

"He don't want your help, teacher lady," James growled in her ear. He threw her away.

She hurtled toward the brick wall. The world went black.

Jerusha Agen

Chapter Nine

*"My face is red with weeping,
and on my eyelids is deep darkness,
although there is no violence in my hands,
and my prayer is pure."*
– Job 16:16-17

A light flashed in the distance. She was in a dark passage. A cave. It was cold, damp. She squinted. There seemed to be a tiny bit of a glow, like a small candle, far down the passage. She walked toward it, unsteadily, the ground beneath her rough and uneven. She put out a hand to steady herself on the wall of the cave but felt only air.

"Miss Sanders?" Dez's voice.

She looked around. Everything was black. She turned back to where she thought she had been headed. The light was gone. Everywhere she turned, she couldn't see anything but blackness. Fear gripped her rapidly beating heart.

"Stop!" A man's voice yelled. The call echoed but couldn't reach her. She would never get out. She was trapped in the dark.

"Has she moved at all?" The woman's voice came from somewhere in the distance.

Mom?

"No. It's only been a few minutes since you left." Nye was there, too. Her voice sounded closer.

Oriana was warm, no longer damp. She must not be in the cave anymore. It had been a dream. She opened her eyes.

At least, she thought she did, but she must not have. Everything was still dark. Maybe she was still dreaming. A pain started at the back of her head, creeping over and around to the front. The discomfort was mild, but seemed to be increasing.

"You should really go home and get some sleep." Nye's hushed tone now sounded very close, as if she were only a couple feet away. "I can stay."

"I don't know," her mom answered.

"Mom, I'll call you as soon as there's a change. You can't do anything here right now."

This dream was almost stranger than the one before. It seemed so ordinary. A dream with her mom and Nye talking in a room. Odd that Oriana wouldn't be involved somehow, but she was like a bug hidden somewhere, just listening. She seemed to be lying on a bed of some sort. A thin sheet or blanket covered her. The dull ache of her head grew stronger.

"Can you really stay? Is Nicanor taking your classes?" Her mom asked.

"I couldn't reach him," Nye said. "I cancelled the ones for today."

Nic. Yes, now Oriana remembered. She had been trying to call him for … what?

Dez. The events of the night came rushing back at once, adding fear to this second dream. What happened? Why couldn't she remember anything after she hit the wall? Why couldn't she wake up?

A steady beeping noise in the background caught her attention. Oh, no. Dread seeped through her body as she recognized the sound that was way too familiar. Weeks spent in a hospital trying to recover from the accident last winter had infused that particular sound with a mix of awful associations that she never wanted to relive. This must be a nightmare.

The pain in her head started to feel like someone was pounding against her skull from the inside. She turned her head, wishing she could wake herself up.

"Oriana?" Nye's voice cut through the darkness.

Thank the Lord. Nye was trying to wake her up. Or was this still part of the dream?

"Oriana, you're awake!"

"Nye?" Oriana rasped.

"Yes, I'm here."

Oriana felt a hand cover her own on top of the blanket.

"Oh, sweetie." Her mom's voice had moved closer. "Thank the Lord."

A hand stroked Oriana's forehead. She knew by feel the hand had to be her mom's. The gesture was normally comforting, but right now it just added to the strangeness of this dream. "Wh—" The word stuck in her dry throat. Her mouth was so parched. She made the effort to swallow. "Where am I?" Her words came out weakly.

There was a pause. "The hospital," Nye finally answered, an odd note in her tone. "I thought you'd recognize the ceiling with all the time you spent here last winter."

Why would Oriana dream something that felt so real, sounded real, and even smelled real? And yet, she couldn't see. She had never had a dream in which she couldn't see. "This is so weird," she whispered to herself.

"What honey?" Her mom sounded like she was right above Oriana's head.

"This dream is weird." Explaining that while in the dream was probably quite pointless.

A longer silence elapsed this time. Silence, except for that grating beep, beep, beep in the background. Oriana noticed that there was something on top of the hand not held by Nye. Probably an IV, if this was supposed to be a hospital.

"This isn't a dream," Nye eventually said. "It probably seems scary to wake up here, but you're okay now. You're safe."

Could people say a dream wasn't one within a dream? Oriana didn't think she had ever encountered that. "Then why can't I see anything?"

That awful silence again. It made her feel disoriented and

lost in the darkness. "Mom? Nye?"

Nye clasped her hand more firmly. "We're here, Oriana."

Someone different suddenly touched her face.

"This is Nurse Jackson, Oriana," Nye thankfully told her, just as Oriana was beginning to panic at the feel of the cold fingers pressing under her eyes.

"Can you see this?" The nurse's voice was deep and scratchy.

"See what?" A nervous apprehension grew as Oriana's mind started to clear. If this was real, why was the room so dark?

Her mother choked back a sob.

"Mom?" Horror crept through Oriana's veins like the coldness of death. "Nye? What's going on? Why is it so dark?"

"Oriana, I ..." Nye stopped when her voice shook.

Nye was never rattled. Something was terribly wrong.

"I think you're blind."

Oriana blinked. She still saw only darkness. She squeezed her eyes shut, hard, then opened them. Darkness. She put her hands over her eyes, not caring that the IV tugged at her skin. She moved her hands away. Darkness.

She screamed.

The scream stabbed like a knife into Nicanor's heart. He jerked away from the door to Oriana's hospital room, where he had quietly listened since the nurse went in and left the door open a few centimeters.

If only he did have a knife, something bigger than the pocket variety he carried with him. Something sharp enough to do the job. He could fall on it and end this misery.

He walked aimlessly down the hallway, his stomach churning with the horror of what he had done. Living with the knowledge that he killed his best friend was almost unbearable. Knowing he was responsible for Oriana … He couldn't go on. The law wouldn't punish him for not answering his cell phone. For not listening to Oriana's message until right after midnight. For being too late to save her from those worthless punks. If only he could, he would give his life to go back and answer her call. The happiest, most loving woman he had known was lying in a hospital, blind. Someone had to pay for that. The thoughts he had after Dante's death swirled in his mind, culminating into the same questions. How could he ever pay for what he had done? How could he go on?

"Nicanor."

He turned to see Nye watching him. He had wandered into the ER waiting room.

There were tracks through her makeup, but her eyes were dry and her gaze as steady as her voice. "Thank you."

He just stared. That was the last thing he expected to hear from her.

"You saved her from so much worse. The police told us you were the one to chase the gang away." She lightly touched his arm. "You saved her life. We are all so grateful. Thank you."

He swallowed. Another secret to hide. More guilt to cover while it slowly choked him. He tried to make himself say the words, to tell her he was responsible for Oriana and for Dante. "She's blind," was all his miserably wretched soul could manage.

"That isn't your fault. We're just so thankful that she's still alive. She will be, too."

Oriana's scream said that was a lie. At least she would know the truth. She would know what Nicanor had done and that her blindness was his fault. She would blame him, as Nye once did for Dante. The thought should make him happy—he would finally get someone's hatred for his guilt. But the idea instead added more weight to his sagging heart. He would never see Oriana smile again.

"She'll get better, Nicanor." Nye nodded gently, as if he were the one who needed comforting.

"The blindness?"

"I don't know ... I hope so. I meant that she'll come around. Oriana's always been the most positive person I know. She'll bounce back and be happier than any of us in no time. You watch. She'll be smiling again before you know it."

Nicanor feared Nye might have absorbed too much of Oriana's naïve optimism. That was the kind of thinking that had made Oriana take such a risk in the first place.

"Nye?" Cullen approached them with Nye's father, who carried fast-food bags. "What happened?" Cullen appeared to be the first to spot the tear tracks on her face.

"She woke up."

"Thank You, Lord." Her father sank into a chair and dropped the bags, the relief apparently hitting his weary body hard.

"But there is some bad news." Nye moistened her lips, looking at the two men.

Now out of Nye's field of vision, Nicanor silently moved away. He didn't need to hear and see more pain. As he reached the exit doors, he couldn't stop himself from looking back.

Cullen held Nye in his arms, while her father was down on one knee. He was weeping or praying. Perhaps both.

Suddenly he no longer saw Oriana's father. He saw his own – falling on his knees, yelling curses at the sky or the God who might be there.

Nicanor backed away from the terrible image until he could force himself to turn and walk out the doors into the black night.

Chapter Ten

*"You have put me in the depths of the pit,
in the regions dark and deep."*
– Psalm 88:6

Two weeks of darkness. That's how long it had been, according to the date Nye told her matched today. Oriana lay on her bed, flat on her back, staring at the darkness that was her world now. Days meant nothing to her anymore. She barely knew where one ended and another began—mornings were as black and horrible as the nights.

Her first few days at home were easier to track, when Nye or her mother had stayed at the apartment overnight. Oriana lay in bed until they got her up, and she ate, or at least sat at the table, when they ate. She couldn't be interested in food with the anxious knot in her chest and constant nausea in the pit of her stomach. Just as well, since she couldn't burn off the calories anymore. Running was on the long list of things she could no longer do. No need to add weight gain to the ugly picture she was sure she made these days.

She couldn't even put on makeup, and she was sure her hair was spiking in every direction. She had tired of trying to brush the unruly waves of her thick hair within the first few days and had Nye cut it super short. Nye said it looked cute, but Oriana knew better. It had to make her look like a guy or extremely ugly. At least she no longer had to try to part the hair evenly and brush out tangles. Her hair was one more thing that wasn't worth the effort.

Just making herself get out of bed in the morning was enough of a challenge. She had never felt this way before, like the blackness all around had seeped inside her, creating a deep, dark pit that was slowly swallowing her soul. This must be what real despair was like. Maybe if she hadn't lived in a fairytale world for so long, she would know what to do now, how to keep living in a world that was so dark.

Why hadn't she just died when she hit the wall? There was no reason to keep living every day, much less to get out of bed when someone told her morning had arrived. She couldn't do anything but bump into things, maybe bruise herself or break something, and be the object of pity from her family. She knew she was taking over Nye's life and her mother's. They took turns at the apartment, serving Oriana the food her mother or church ladies had made and stockpiled in the refrigerator. Nye made sure Oriana got dressed, washed, could find her toothpaste and toothbrush, made it out of the bathroom without a huge mess—all the things any toddler would need.

Her mother and Nye even chose clothes to lay out for Oriana at night before they left, supposedly putting together a coordinated outfit for her to wear the next day. The effort was pointless, since it didn't matter what she wore. She wasn't going anywhere.

"Oriana," Nye called, from the kitchen, Oriana guessed. "Breakfast is almost ready."

If she were able to laugh, the reversal in their roles would be funny. Oriana used to be the one waking Nye up, dragging her out of bed with what Nye called "annoying perkiness."

With a grunt, Oriana slowly rolled onto her side and lowered her feet to the cold faux wood floor. Soft carpeting in the room would be so much nicer, but it would probably make it harder to keep her balance anyway.

She felt for her nightstand before she stood up. Using that to orient her as best she could, she started to walk around the bed, keeping close enough to feel the mattress brushing her leg.

Pain hit her foot. "Ow!" She lifted it with a grimace. She must have stubbed her toe on the leg of the bed again. The poor toe had to be black and blue from the many times she had jammed it on furniture. Her mother wanted her to wear shoes all the time, but the clearer feeling from bare feet allowed her to tell where she was and balance better.

"Are you okay?"

She jerked at the nearness of Nye's voice. Oriana must have exclaimed louder than she thought. "I'll live, if that's what you mean." She continued around the end of the bed to its other corner, which she felt with her hands. She let go and walked toward where the chair should be, waving her hands in the air in front of her.

"Left."

Oriana stopped. She hated that. The audience when she didn't know it. Always being watched, and she could never see her watchers.

"The chair is farther to your left."

"If you're going to just stand there, why don't you hand me the clothes?" Oriana snapped. "Unless you're having too much fun watching me stumble around."

"No, I'm not." Nye's walk even sounded graceful, her steps light as she flowed into the room. "Here's your sweater."

Oriana grasped the soft material Nye pressed in her hand. It felt like wool.

"It's your green turtleneck sweater. I've paired it with your at-home jeans," she added, referring to Oriana's comfortable, broken-in jeans with holes on the knees that she saved for weekends at home.

Oriana always wore a shirt under the turtleneck, since the wool made her itch, but she supposed it didn't matter. Discomforts of all kinds came with this torture. The scratchiness might add some interest to another day of monotonous darkness. At least she would know she was awake.

"Today, I'll start on your drawers and closet. If we group everything in order of type and color, you should be able to pick out your own outfits."

Just like a big girl, Oriana finished sarcastically in her head.

"Do you have a preference which drawer I put what in?"

"It doesn't matter, Nye." Oriana didn't keep the irritation out of her tone. Did Nye really think such trivial things were somehow going to make her life all happy and bright again?

Nye sighed. "Can you finish here? I should check the toast."

"Sure." She waited until she heard the door close before she started to remove her pajamas. At least she could still change in private—she hoped.

Panic churned in her stomach. As far as she knew, the curtains on the window could be open right now. "Nye!"

"Are you okay?" Nye's voice drew closer through the door.

"Are the curtains closed?"

"In your room?"

No, in the living room. "Yes!"

"They're closed. I checked."

Oriana breathed again.

"Are you okay?"

"Yes." No.

"Okay, let me know if you need help."

She needed help all right. She needed someone to wake her up from this nightmare.

Oriana somehow managed to dress herself and, with only two bumps into walls, reached the dining area by the open kitchen, where the smell of eggs, toast, and bacon wafted toward her.

"Good, you made it."

Oriana noted the surprise in her sister's tone. Oriana couldn't tell half the time if her family wanted her to be helpless or just expected her to be. The sickening truth was that she was helpless and always would be. She might as well get used to it.

Oriana was sure she was being watched as she felt around for the chair, not knowing how close she was to the table.

"Careful." Nye grabbed Oriana's arm. "You almost hit the plate. Your chair's over here." She gently pulled Oriana to the chair, which she fumbled to feel. "Here." The chair scraped on the floor as Nye pulled it out. "It's behind you. Just sit down."

She made herself start to sit. Her stomach dropped like she was falling just before she landed on the chair. She felt sick again.

"Should I pray?"

"Are you eating?"

"No, I ate at home with Cullen."

"Then I think I can manage it on my own." Oriana closed her eyes, a silly habit since it made no difference now. Strange that she had needed darkness to focus on prayer before. Now that she was in constant darkness, she couldn't seem to pray at all. The only words that ever came to mind were simple: Why? What had she done wrong? But she knew better than to ask God those questions. Mature Christians didn't ask why.

And she knew it would be silly to blame Him for what happened. She had watched Nye do that for three years when she lost Dante and had learned the lesson of her sister's experience well. God knew what He was doing when he allowed Dante's accident, just like when he had allowed her car crash last winter. He brought good even out of Dante's death.

But her blindness was no accident. Evil, dark people were to blame—the darkness Oriana had underestimated, thinking she could fix it with some smiles and kindness. Evil people. That was her answer to the "why" question. Such evil was so much worse than she had ever let herself believe existed in her fairytale world. Even a little boy she had loved could do something so terrible—

The image of Dez, watching while James choked her with his arm and breathed on her face, flashed in her mind. She gasped and opened her eyes to the darkness. A jolt of fear surged in her stomach. There was nothing to make the images of her mind go away anymore. Only darkness.

"Are you okay?" Nye was watching again.

Why did people keep asking her that? Oriana wished she could glare at her sister, but she didn't know where to turn her head. "No, I'm not okay."

There was no quick response like Oriana had expected.

Nye was no doubt trying to keep from arguing with the invalid. It wouldn't be fair. "You're probably just hungry," she said at last. "Do you want me to help you?"

"I'm blind, Nye. Food won't fix that."

"I didn't mean that." She sounded so calm.

Since when had Nye developed the patience of a saint? Irritation added to the curdling of Oriana's stomach. This great restraint only came out of pity.

"I just meant that you need your strength. Shall I cut up the bacon?"

"I'm not hungry." Oriana hated the five-year-old tone to her words.

"Okay." The refrigerator door opened. "Maybe some juice. I forgot to get it out."

Oriana bit her tongue. Let Nye have her moment of service.

"So," Nye started in a cheerful tone, "you haven't mentioned Nicanor at all for a long time."

Nic. She didn't let herself think about him, let alone talk about him. "Is he still around?" Her lips tugged into a cynical sneer. "I thought sure he would've run back to New York by now."

"No, he's still here." Nye made noises on the counter, probably with the jug and glass. "He's been helping out at the studio when I'm here."

"Nice of him to do that." Oriana didn't try to hide the sarcasm in the words. So even Nic was involved in the charity case of her existence. Wonderful.

"He saved your life, Oriana."

Oriana turned her head in the general direction of her sister's voice. "I know." Oriana bit her lip. "I didn't mean anything against him. I'm very grateful." Not grateful to be alive with this blindness but thankful that those creeps hadn't been able to do whatever else they planned. How could she ever have been so stupid as to think she could help such cruel, terrible people? She would have to learn the hard way that they were lost beyond reach.

"He asks about you every day."

"He does?" Oriana couldn't keep the pleasant surprise out of her voice, and probably showed the reaction on her face, too.

"Like clockwork. Maybe you could have him over sometime. I think he would really like to see you."

The idea of Nic seeing her like this was almost as horrifying as the darkness she was staring at. He probably only wanted to come out of pity or curiosity anyway. That's all she'd ever be to any man now.

Nye came to the table and set what sounded like a glass on it. "Would you want to?"

"Sure, why not?" Bitterness saturated her response. "Bring another person to the freak show. Even Cullen's been given a view."

"I'm sorry that bothered you, but I didn't know it would." The frustration in Nye's voice didn't sound apologetic. "He just wanted to see how you were doing. If you want to get better at things, why don't you work with that orientation and mobility specialist mother told you about?"

"No, thank you." Oriana shook her head. Another person around to watch the humiliation? A stranger? Having her family see her like this was bad enough.

"Why not?"

"There's no point. I'm not going anywhere."

"You could if you learned how."

"I don't want to, Nye," she snapped.

Nye was quiet a moment. "Will you drink your juice?" Nye took Oriana's hand and placed it on the cold glass.

Oriana jerked back. "I don't want any."

"Oriana, stop!" Nye finally lost her saintly patience. "Are you really going to refuse to eat and drink for the rest of your life?"

"Why not?" Oriana's voice rose. "I can't live like this."

"Well I can't stand to see you moping around and feeling sorry for yourself all the time."

"That's funny. I watched you do it for three years!"

Silence.

Oriana swallowed past the taste of guilt rising in her throat. She listened closely.

Nye sniffed. Was she crying? Nye didn't cry. Certainly not from an argument. Another strange noise. Then it sounded like Nye dashed from the room.

Oriana got up and followed as fast as she could manage, thankful, for once, that the apartment was small. She found the hallway soon enough and went toward the retching sounds coming from the bathroom. The toilet flushed when Oriana reached the doorway. She reached out to confirm the door was still open. "Did you just throw up?"

The faucet started running. "Sorry I got emotional. I hate it. Poor Cullen has to put up with this all the time."

"You have morning sickness." Oriana felt ill herself. She hadn't thought even once of Nye's pregnancy since she woke up to this terrible darkness. She had forgotten her own sister was pregnant.

"Yes."

A rush of realizations, each of them increasingly painful, washed over Oriana. She wouldn't see Nye change as she went through the pregnancy. She would never see her own niece or nephew. She would never know what the baby looked like, or as it grew into a child, and an adult. She would probably not even be able to play with the little boy or girl, or babysit, or be the wonderful aunt she had wanted to be. And what about children of her own? It was too awful to think about, too awful to bear.

"Go home, Nye." Oriana turned away from the doorway

and felt her way along the wall to her bedroom, she hoped.

"What?" Nye said from behind, apparently following.

"You shouldn't be here when you're sick. I didn't know you were."

"I can't leave you alone."

"Nye," Oriana's voice was sharp as she abruptly stopped and turned toward her sister's direction. "I'm still an adult, and I'm telling you to leave me alone. Go home. Take care of yourself for a change."

Oriana could almost hear the clicking of Nye's brain in the silence. Oriana clenched her jaw and waited, ready for a fight if she got one.

"Mother will be here later this afternoon," Nye finally stated. "Or maybe she said evening. I better call and check."

"I can do that if I want to." If she could find the phone, that is. Ever the smart one, Nye had programmed the first three buttons of Oriana's cell with important phone numbers in case of emergency. "Go, Nye. I want to be alone."

"That's not always the best thing, even when you want it. Like you said, I should know."

Oriana swallowed. "I'm sorry I said that," she managed.

"I'm sorry, too."

"Now go home and take care of your baby."

"Okay." The word was heavy with reluctance as Nye finally turned to leave. She called out a few final assurances and directions before she exited, but Oriana paid them no heed.

The change in Oriana's life had apparently been the key to activating Nye's mothering instincts. Or maybe the little one growing inside her sister had created the transformation.

Oriana sighed when she heard the door close. Now she had two mothers. Or was it three? Mrs. Peters was making too many visits with food and sweets, as well. Oriana stumbled over to her bed. She stretched out on it, settling in to sleep and trying not to think as she awaited the arrival of the next mother.

Jerusha Agen

Chapter Eleven

"Are not my days few?
Then cease, and leave me alone,
that I may find a little cheer
before I go—and I shall not return—
to the land of darkness and deep shadow,
the land of gloom like thick darkness,
like deep shadow without any order,
where light is as thick as darkness."
– Job 10:20-22

Nicanor saw Nye standing at the back of the dance floor as the adult students clapped and went out of the room. She smiled at the women as they left, but Nicanor could tell from the lines on her forehead as she approached him that she wasn't happy. "I need to talk to you."

"Oriana? She is alright?"

"No, she isn't."

His heart started to race. "Did they find the men?" His throat was dry.

"No, no." She looked at his face, as if she just noticed the concern that gripped him. "I'm sorry, I didn't mean to make you think that. Officer Kelly said they still haven't found Dez or his brother, but she's safe right now. We haven't told her about the danger." She took a deep breath. "But she's not at all well. She's not herself anymore. Not the Oriana we used to know."

He breathed again but felt the heaviness of Nye's words.

"She sent me away, and my mother said she had the same attitude with her yesterday. She doesn't smile or laugh. I know this whole thing is hard, of course, but … it's something more than that." Nye looked away. When she turned back, a single tear was sliding down her cheek.

Nicanor stared at the tear. He had never seen her cry before. Regret twisted his stomach. He had caused this.

"I think she's given up on living. It's like she's in some black hole, and I can't reach her. Neither can my parents." She lifted her eyes to meet his gaze. "I'm hoping you can."

He just stared at her, not sure what she meant and hoping she didn't mean what he thought.

"Will you go and see her?"

She did mean that. Part of him wanted to say "yes," and sprint out the door, rushing to see Oriana and make amends somehow. His smarter side knew the truth—he didn't want to see what he had done to her. He couldn't bear it. And he could not face the hatred she probably had for him now.

"You're the only one who might be able to help her. Please, Nicanor." Nye's voice dropped to a whisper as another tear fell. "I don't want to lose her."

He swallowed. He had to go.

Forty minutes later, Nicanor put his hands in the pockets of his jacket as he pressed into the cold wind, walking the block from the bus stop to Oriana's apartment. He should have thought of what he would say by now, but nothing that came to him sounded right. Dread gripped him as he walked. What if she really did hate him for not saving her from this? He deserved it, but he didn't know if he could take it—a glare or fierce frown instead of that smile and sparkling eyes.

"Remember that she's different," Nye had warned him, just before she shooed him out the door.

Imagining anything other than the happy Oriana he had known this short time was difficult. He wondered what Nye expected from him. Cheering people up had never been a talent he possessed, but she should know that. Yet she was still convinced he could help, or perhaps she was just that desperate.

"She really needs someone with her every day," Nye had added, anxiety obvious in her tone. "I'll find a way to manage all the classes here, if you need to be there."

The look on Nicanor's face must have given away the panic that sparked inside him at her pressured hinting. He wasn't even sure he could make himself go there once.

"But I'm grateful for whatever you can do." Nye had quickly backtracked. "If you can stay a while today, until my mother gets there tonight, that would be a great start."

A start. Nicanor ducked his head as the wind struck his face. The idea of going one time to see a woman who likely hated him was daunting enough. He couldn't help her. This visit wasn't a start to anything. If not for Nye's tears, he wouldn't even be trying today. But he could not choose to hurt Nye more than he already had.

So here he was, slowly walking to the home of the other woman he had hurt and now owed a debt he could never repay. He replayed that evening over and over again in his head, his stomach churning when he thought of how he had sat on the mattress in his apartment, an unopened bottle of whiskey in his hand as the phone vibrated on the counter. The only reason he was awake to hear the call was because he was saving his last two doses of sleeping pills for when he most needed them. He had no money to buy more.

It didn't matter. He ignored the call, as he always did. Three times, he let it go. The last message Terry had left included several choice words for his former dancing star, and Nicanor thought the new calls were more of the same. He didn't know it was Oriana. She had never called before. Would he have answered if he had seen she was the caller? He might have. If only he could go back.

The story of his life. Always making the worst of mistakes and having to live with not being able to undo them. His father was right—he was worthless.

Nicanor stopped at the end of the path that led to the apartment building. The clean, new structure made of red brick and stone made Nicanor's apartment building look like a decayed rabbit hutch by comparison. He took out a cigarette and lit it up, taking a few drags under the cloudy skies of midday. Their color suggested snow.

He still hadn't thought of a word to say or even how to act when he saw Oriana. The cigarette bought him more time to figure it out. Too soon, the cigarette was through and so was his time. He smashed the butt under his shoe and headed for the door.

"You're the only one who might be able to help her," Nye had said.

Despite the depressing reality that stared him in the face, something positive, almost like hope, sparked in Nicanor as he remembered Nye's words. Perhaps this was his chance. He could never pay for Dante or for Oriana's blindness, but if Nye were right, if he could at least help in some small way, it would be the miracle he was looking for. If he really could do something for Oriana, he needed no encouragement or pleadings to do it.

He pressed the buzzer for her apartment and waited.

Nothing.

He reached to press again when the front door suddenly swung open.

A short, older woman with bright red hair held the door, a

smile creasing her round face with well-used folds and wrinkles. "Come on in." She beckoned for him to enter.

He grabbed the door so she could step away and went inside. A straight hallway greeted him, with the door of the first apartment open.

"You must be here to see Oriana." The woman smiled, as if unaware she was psychic.

He stared blankly at her.

"I'm Bernadette Peters," she said, apparently to explain.

He was still missing something.

She laughed. "Nye called and told me you were coming. I go to church with the girls."

And had for some time, judging from her description of the very grownup Sanders women.

"I'm so glad to hear Oriana has a man who can watch over her right now. Oh, I know." She lifted a hand to stop him, though he made no protest. "Nye said you're just friends, but Oriana so needs a strong man to protect her and take care of everything. My Albert was a rock in times like these."

"I'm sure he was." Agreement seemed like the fastest way to end the conversation.

"Now you go ahead and run up to see Oriana. She's probably lonely by now. I stop by with some goodies now and then, but I try not to interfere too much. Poor thing." She pointed to the staircase to the left of the door. "She's right up there, sweetie."

He reached the stairs in two strides.

"You are staying for a while?"

He paused. "I don't know."

"Well, you stop by for some cookies if you leave before I get them up there." She made a shooing motion with her hand. "She shouldn't be left alone now so you go on up."

He started up the steps, and Mrs. Peters disappeared behind the wall that separated the staircase from the hall. Strange that she trusted him so much. She looked like the type to say he shouldn't be alone with Oriana in her apartment. Perhaps Nye's recommendation carried that much weight.

Nicanor took a deep breath as he reached Oriana's door on the first landing. He had no plans, but it seemed he was trapped. He had to knock.

No response.

He rapped again, harder. He waited a minute.

Still not a sound.

He tried again, his breath quickening. From what Nye said, he knew Oriana wouldn't have gone out. Something was wrong. She wasn't herself, depressed. What if she had done something about it? The Oriana he knew wouldn't do that, but Nye said she had changed.

Or what if the kid and his banger brother had found her? Horrible possibilities raced through Nicanor's mind with the thought.

He whipped out his pocket knife and inserted the small

blade into the lock of the door. He would protect her this time. The lock released, and he quietly opened the door, sure his thumping heart beat would give him away if there was anyone inside.

He could see the open living room, kitchen, and small dining table at once. The connected areas of the large apartment were bathed in light that came through glass balcony doors. The colorful greens and blues of the walls seemed to laugh at Nicanor's fears with their cheery perkiness. But if nothing was wrong, where was Oriana?

The ticking of a wall clock above the dining table was the only sound. Nicanor quietly turned down the short hallway to his right. He approached the first doorway.

A small bathroom. Empty.

There was one more door at the end of the hall. Closed.

He carefully turned the doorknob and opened it, slowly, without a sound. The room was dim, the thin shades drawn. A chair sat near the door and a large bed farther in. Someone was lying on it.

He silently went to the bed.

Oriana. Fully clothed in jeans and a sweater, she lay on top of the twisted sheets as if sleeping deeply.

His chest began to ache as he watched her. It seemed so long, so very long since he last saw her. He hadn't remembered her being quite so beautiful. Her hair had been cut short, but the change seemed to reveal more loveliness—the high cheekbones and smooth skin of her oval face, the full lips and long, dark eyelashes that brushed her pale cheeks.

His gaze moved to the nightstand beside her where a small pill bottle rested, the lid removed and sitting beside it. His heartbeat quickened. He crouched and gently grasped her wrist.

"Oriana." He searched for a pulse. "Oriana."

She moaned and turned her head toward him, her eyes still shut.

There, he felt it. Her pulse beneath the soft skin was strong, normal.

"Oriana, wake up." His own heartbeat calmed as he looked at her, feeling something more than relief that she seemed safe. He gently brushed her jagged bangs away from her eyebrows.

Her eyes opened. The large brown orbs stared right at his face, but looked like they were watching something else, farther away.

She jerked back and sat up. "Who's there? Who is it?"

"Oriana, you're safe." The stark fear on her face felt like a slash in his side. "It's only Nicanor."

"Nicanor?" she whispered, her breathing quick and uneven.

"I'm sorry I frightened you." And sorry for so much more.

"Wha—What are you doing here?" She looked at the wall ahead of her, or aimed her eyes there.

Somehow he couldn't remember that she could no longer see. "Nye sent me."

"Nye."

He couldn't read her expression, especially when he could only see one side of her face.

"How did you get in here?" Her voice was pitched lower than he remembered. Her tone was grim, weary, with a note of something else that was new. Suspicion.

"You didn't answer when I knocked." He stood as he searched for some excuse for his overreaction when she didn't answer the door. How could he explain it to her? He couldn't explain it to himself. Taking action at all, much less charging in to save someone was foreign to him. "Then I saw the pills on your nightstand."

She tilted her head higher, toward his face. "On my ..." her furrowed brow changed to narrowed eyes as she continued, "and you thought what, exactly?"

He said nothing, stunned by the sharpness of her voice.

"That I tried to kill myself? Just what did Nye tell you about me?"

There it was—what he had dreaded to see. Disgust. Anger. She did hate him. He walked around the bed and stopped at the door. "I'm sorry."

She jerked her head toward his new location.

"I'll leave you alone." He left the room and walked down the hallway. He reached the apartment door.

"Nicanor!" Oriana called from the bedroom. "Ow!" she exclaimed at the same time he heard a thud.

He rushed back.

She stood by the chair, her hand on its back as she held up her foot.

"Are you hurt?"

She lowered her foot, her wince fading. "Thank you for not asking if I was alright."

He hadn't meant to avoid that question, but he understood. The few friends he used to have, his dance partners, his agent—they all must have asked him that question a thousand times, and a thousand times Nicanor had lied and said he was fine. That response was all they wanted to hear.

"I'm sorry I got mad at you. You scared me, and I was angry at my sister. It has nothing to do with you."

He studied the face that was turned toward him. The flashing anger had left her eyes, leaving only stark despair in the brown pools. Nye was right. Oriana was deep in a black hole. Nicanor should know—he had lived in one for all but seven years of his life. Oriana didn't belong there. But a person in the same pit could never be the one to help her out.

"Did Nye ask you to visit me?"

"Yes," he answered, without thinking.

Her frown deepened. "I'm sorry she made you do that. You didn't have to come."

"She didn't make me."

"She didn't." Her eyes narrowed with the skeptical statement.

He watched her for a moment. "Do you want me to leave?" He braced himself, not sure which answer he hoped for.

She shifted as if she was going to let go of the chair, then leaned on it again. "I'd offer you some coffee or something, but you probably know I can't do that. I assume Nye told you how helpless I am." Bitterness edged her voice like a sharp blade.

"I'll have some."

"What?" Confusion broke through the cynicism for a moment.

"Coffee."

"Oh." She waited, as if expecting him to say something else. "Okay," she eventually said. Her eyebrows dipped together as she hesitantly let go of the chair and walked toward Nicanor.

He stepped aside as she came closer, her outstretched hand almost brushing his jacket sleeve.

"Do you smoke?" she suddenly asked.

"Sometimes." Not enough to get the smell, or so he thought. Must be on the jacket.

"I never noticed before," she murmured to herself, as she felt her way down the hall.

He took off his jacket and followed a few feet behind her.

"I thought dancers weren't supposed to smoke." She

spoke more loudly this time, still turned away.

The reminder of Dante's usual phrase was another jab to Nicanor's wounded psyche. "You're right," he managed to say.

"Are you watching me?" She reached the end of the hall and tilted her head toward her shoulder.

He could easily lie, but he didn't want to add that to his list of sins. "Yes."

She turned to face straight ahead. "I'd rather you didn't."

"All right." He had no idea where he was supposed to look instead.

She followed the turn of the wall to the little dining area before the kitchen.

Nicanor walked out of the hallway and crossed to the living room in an effort to respect her wishes. He set his jacket on the arm of the sofa, which was a bold red color.

"Ouch."

He looked to see her slide a chair, the apparent offender, further under the table.

"Where are you?" A hint of panic touched her voice as she turned her head in multiple directions.

"Here. By the sofa."

"Look, you're going to have to talk more, Nicanor. You're even quieter than Nye when you move, and I can't read your expressions anymore." Frustration and bitterness hung on the words as she shot them out. "As if I ever could."

"I thought it was 'Nic.'"

She turned her head away.

Was she remembering that day she had called him Nic? The day before the terrible night. He hadn't meant to bring all that up. "I—"

"Hello!" The cheery voice and soft rap at the door saved him from needing to cover for his mistake. A perfect cap of flat red curls appeared around the door, followed by the round, smiling face of Mrs. Peters. "Good, you found each other!" She pushed the door open fully and entered, carrying a plate stacked with cookies. "Your door was open, Oriana." The little woman bustled into the kitchen, clearly familiar with the apartment.

"Was it." Another rhetorical statement of disinterest. Oriana shifted the chair she was still gripping and pulled it out, apparently intending to sit.

"Yes, dear. That's not really the safest thing, and there were scratches on the keyhole of your doorknob. I'll have to see the landlord about that."

Nicanor cringed inwardly. It wouldn't take much for Oriana to realize how he had gotten in, unless she was distracted, as he was, by wondering why Mrs. Peters had looked at Oriana's keyhole.

"I'm so glad you're up and about today," Mrs. Peters continued after a quick breath. "You'll get better in no time that way. Oh, here, let me help you." She hustled around the counter to reach Oriana just as she sat down in the chair. "Oh, you did it! Good girl. I knew you would get the hang of things."

A pink flush colored Oriana's cheeks. Whether from anger or embarrassment, Nicanor couldn't tell.

"Now, Nicanor—is that right, Nicanor?" Mrs. Peters glanced at him as she rushed back to the kitchen. "Such a striking name. Would you like some coffee ... or tea?"

"I was getting him some." Oriana's tone was sullen as she glared at the table, her back rigid.

"Oh." Mrs. Peters stared at Oriana with widened eyes. Then her smile popped back up, and she went over to Oriana at the table. "There, you see? You never could find a young man to have over 'til this happened. I can see he's been good for you already." She patted Oriana's shoulder, making her start. "Romans 8:28, dear, remember?" Mrs. Peters smiled at Nicanor, clearly not noticing that Oriana looked as if she might explode under that patting hand.

"What kind of cookies did you bring?" Nicanor couldn't care less, but he had to say something to diffuse the situation.

"Hmm? Oh, I brought Oriana's favorite. Oatmeal raisin."

"Wonderful." Nicanor headed for Mrs. Peters as casually as he could. "You must be a very good baker."

She laughed. "Well, my Albert thought so. And the Sanders girls have always loved my cookies, isn't that right, Oriana?"

"Wonderful." Nicanor reached Mrs. Peters' side and

gently took her arm, as he smoothly guided her toward the door. "Thank you for bringing those. We'll return you the plate when it's empty, which I'm sure won't be long." He ushered her out the door. "Goodbye." He waved as he closed the door, leaving her blinking with surprise, but still smiling.

The apartment was as quiet as the calm after a storm.

"I've never heard you talk like that." Oriana's head turned in his direction.

"Like what?" he said, remembering to speak as he walked over to the table.

"So … I don't know. Charming, I guess."

He stopped and stood on the other side of the table from where she sat. "I see." Most people didn't think he could be nice. Why did it bother him that she also thought of him that way?

"Thanks for your help."

"You're welcome."

They stayed silent a moment.

Oriana broke the silence. "You're supposed to talk now, remember?"

Great. Gone were the days when she would do all the talking, apparently. He tried to think of something to say. If she wanted him to talk, then she shouldn't take offense if he wanted to understand what just happened. "Mrs. Peters said something about the Romans. What did she mean?"

Oriana sighed and propped her elbow on the table to lean

her head on her hand. "Not 'the Romans.' Romans 8:28. It's a Bible verse about tough times."

Dante used to quote the Bible to Nicanor occasionally. He didn't remember that verse. "What does it say?"

"And we know that in all things God works for the good of those who love Him, who have been called according to His purpose," she recited in a flat tone, pressing her forehead into her hand.

He would have remembered that one if he had heard it. What an incredible, crazy thing to believe. God working *everything* out for good—everything for the people who love Him, at least. Perhaps that was Nicanor's problem. He hadn't loved God since he was seven, and he knew he wasn't called by Him. Yet Oriana loved God and still ended up here, blind because she was kind to someone. Or did it mean good was supposed to come out of her blindness? He gripped the back of the chair in front of him. "Do you believe that?"

"Of course." She lifted her head, her brow furrowed.

"But you didn't want Mrs. Peters to say it?" He never asked such personal questions, but Oriana's reaction to Mrs. Peters just did not make sense if she believed that verse. It would be an amazing guarantee, a hope too good to be true.

"No ... It's complicated. Just something between Christians, I guess. The verse gets misused a lot. Thrown around like a bandage that's supposed to make everything better."

He wanted to ask her more, but her abrupt tone signaled that she didn't want to talk about it.

"Do you still want coffee?" she asked, after another long pause.

"Do you?"

"No."

"Then neither do I." He kept the relief out of his voice. He never drank coffee—only strong espresso when he had the money for it. But he would down Oriana's coffee if it meant keeping her from feeling helpless.

"She was right, you know."

He watched her, then remembered she couldn't see him waiting for her to explain. "Mrs. Peters?"

"Yes. I can't really make coffee, for you or myself."

"Neither can I." He pulled out the chair and sat opposite her.

Her gaze shifted to aim at his chin. "That's not what I meant."

"I know."

She stared for a moment. "Why are you here, Nicanor?"

"Ny—"

"Nye sent you, I know. I mean, why are you here, in Harper? Why aren't you in New York? Nye says you have a great career going."

He looked down at the table and slid his finger along the grain of the wood. "Had."

"What happened?"

He stood, restless. He walked into the living room.

"Nicanor?" The note of anxiety returned to her voice as she tilted her head.

"Sorry." He covered the ten feet to go back to the table. "I forgot to talk."

The corner of her mouth pulled up just slightly as her other features relaxed. "It's okay."

Was that the tiny start of a smile? Seeing the hope of one made him realize how much he missed the real thing, with the sparkle in those eyes that were now so dark and painful. What could he do to make her smile?

"You didn't answer my question."

He had hoped she wouldn't notice.

"What happened?"

He narrowed his eyes at her. The new Oriana was painfully direct. "I came here."

"Okay." She crossed her arms. "Then we're back to the first question. Why are you here?"

He watched her, the furrowed brow forming new lines that peaked out from under her angled bangs, the question mixed with pain in her eyes. "To pay a debt." His words were quiet, scaring him with their stark honesty. He half hoped she wouldn't hear him.

She lowered her arms, the lines disappearing as her eyebrows went up. Her mouth opened, then closed.

"Why are *you* here?" He had to stop the interrogation somehow.

She fiddled with a short clump of hair at the side of her head. "Because I love ... loved Harper. I loved the kids." Her voice caught. She moistened her lips. "I thought I could make a difference." Her tone became hard with the words as she lowered her hand and stared, as if at the table.

"There are other children in your class."

She did smile this time, but only in a sardonic, humorless display of pain. "I don't have a class. I'll never have another class, and it's a good thing, since I obviously didn't know what I was doing." Pools of moisture glistened in her dark eyes. "They were right. Everyone who always said I was in over my head. 'Sweet little Oriana is too naïve to handle those kids,'" she quoted in a mocking tone as the tears tumbled over and ran down her cheeks.

He wanted to go to her and wipe those tears away, but how could he when he knew he had thought as much himself? He was one of those people who believed she was out of her depth. Guilty again.

"Well," she sniffed and swiped at the tears, "they were right. I had no idea what I was dealing with. That a little boy could be so terrible. And his brother ... " She shuddered.

He pulled out the chair opposite her again and sat down. "You're safe now."

"Safe?" She lifted her face, her eyes searching for him.

"I'll never be safe. I never was." The last words fell to a whisper as she dropped her gaze.

He wanted to touch the hand she rested on the table, but he was afraid he would startle her. "They will be caught."

"It won't change what they did. No punishment they get would pay for ... this." She gestured with her hand to her eyes.

His breath left him. *She* could say that. Cheerful, forgiving Oriana. If there was no hope for Dez and his brother, there was no hope for Nicanor. They had taken a woman's sight. Nicanor had taken his only friend's life.

"I'll keep you safe." He stared at her sightless eyes as his mind screamed at him to make amends somehow. "I won't let them hurt you."

"They already did."

The words twisted the knife in his heart. "I'm sorry."

"No apologies. Remember?"

She used his words, but he couldn't tell if she meant them to hurt him as much as they did. "I should have gone with you," he whispered.

"Nicanor." She extended her hand across the table, as if reaching for him.

He slid his hand forward, until she found where he was and laid her fingers gently on his forearm.

"It wasn't your fault. You came as soon as you could, and I'm eternally grateful that you did." She drew her hand back. "*They* did this to me." Her gaze lowered. "Some people can't be reached, no matter how hard we try." Her voice faded on the last words, and she turned her head slightly away. Her eyes filled with despair, as if she were seeing the horizon of a hopeless world.

He had looked on that same horizon for far too long. Why did a woman so innocent and happy have to end up in such darkness? And the worthless punks who made her like that were getting off free. Was there never justice in this world?

She was right. He couldn't guarantee her safety, but he could see that the thugs who did this to her did not go unpunished. If she wouldn't acknowledge his fault, he would find the others and make sure they paid. That had to make a difference.

※

Oriana had seen the shadow over Nicanor before—that darkness reflected in his grim face and sullen expression. Now, she could feel it. Or was she sensing her own? Knowing where one stopped and the other began was a challenge.

She thought she would be nervous knowing that the handsome Nicanor was watching her, even now sitting across from her at the table, when she couldn't see him and knew she looked a mess herself. Instead, she felt more relaxed than she had ever been in his presence, as if she shared a strange new kinship with him. She felt a certainty that, of all the people she knew, he was the only one who could possibly understand her situation.

She wasn't sure why she believed that. After all, he had no disability and was still extremely different from her. He was likely still as perfect-looking as before, but that mattered little now in her dark world. Voices were more important, and his was very pleasant to listen to. The deep, even cadence matched his accent perfectly, especially when he said her name.

When she woke up with him touching her wrist and saying "Oriana," rolling the "r" every time, she thought she was dreaming. Remembering that the darkness around her was real was enough to yank her out of the romantic notion. This blindness was at least good for ending any delusions of romance and fantasy. Nicanor may still be able to send a shiver up her spine, but he was only there because Nye begged him to come.

A lack of feeling on his side would be best anyway. He was from a different world than she was—that somber world she had just begun to know and couldn't face. She had the feeling his childhood was as bad as the lives of the street kids in her classes. He was even a smoker, she reminded herself, continuing the list of cons. Lest she forget, she was also blind—the greatest insurmountable obstacle of all. If she had little chance with a guy like Nicanor before, she had zero now.

And, he wasn't a Christian.

She grabbed a short little clump of hair and rolled it

between her fingers.

He was just sitting there.

Was he watching her? She wished she knew. She felt the warmth of his presence and heard the soft sound of his breathing. The clock on the wall ticked in the background. Funny how she had never noticed it made a noise before. "How long are you supposed to stay?"

"Do you want me to go?" he countered in that velvety voice. He kept doing that—answering her question with a question. Annoying, but, for some reason, it didn't irritate her as much as if Nye or her mother had done the same thing. She felt different with Nicanor. She was relaxed, her nerves not so constantly on edge. An odd change, since she had always been fluttery and nervous around him in the past.

Still, two could play the game he started. "Did you pick my lock?" See how he liked having his questions unanswered. She was getting used to waiting for the pause that almost always came before he spoke, but she had to wait a moment longer than usual this time. If only she could see if she had made him squirm with the question. A nervous Nicanor would be a sight.

"Yes," he eventually answered.

"That's how you got into the classroom at school, too, isn't it?"

"Yes."

Mystery solved. "I knew I hadn't left it unlocked." She

had spent days double checking that she really locked rooms at the school after that. How curious that he would go around picking locks whenever he wanted to get in somewhere. "Where did you learn how to do that?" He might not be keen on personal questions, but he was here, in her apartment and in her life when everything was deeply personal. She needed to even the playing field. A psychiatrist would no doubt identify what she was doing as an effort to offset her feeling of vulnerability. That would probably be right.

"Argentina."

"When you were young?"

"Yes."

What kind of boy learned to pick locks as casually as Nicanor did? Actually, she didn't have to work hard to picture any one of her students learning the same type of thing. "Your childhood was pretty rough, wasn't it?"

"I survived."

"Will you tell me about it?"

He tensed in the silence.

At least, she thought she felt him tense, but she might have imagined the change. "We have lots of time to kill. If you want to stay. I'm afraid all I can do these days is talk and listen."

He cleared his throat and shifted in the chair. "What is it that you want to know?"

She shrugged and leaned against the spindly back of the wooden chair. "What were your parents like?"

There was a long pause. Oriana was about to speak when he finally started to talk.

"My mother was ... beautiful, soft ... gentle. Like an angel in a dream."

Moisture pricked Oriana's eyes at the sadness and longing in his voice. He sounded like a little boy, lost and alone. "Is she gone?" Oriana gently asked, though his words had given her the answer.

"Yes."

"When did it happen?"

"I was seven."

"I'm so sorry."

They were silent again. The clock ticked as Oriana visualized a young Nic, the little boy lost in Argentina. "Did you have your father still?"

"He's alive, yes." The change in Nicanor's voice was as different as night and day used to be.

"You don't get along." From his grim tone, Oriana was sure enough to turn the question into a statement.

"He cannot forgive me."

"Forgive you for what?"

"For living."

Her brow furrowed as she tried to make sense of that.

"There are worse stories." He shifted in the chair again. "Perhaps your children?"

Her children. She used to call her students that. She had felt as if they were her kids in many ways. His words brought their faces to mind, images and memories that seemed to come from an age ago, a different life. "Some." She thought of their backgrounds and volatile homes. "Most of them come from single parent families. Maria's mother died when she was three, so she lives with her father. The rest of the kids are all living with their mothers, but two of them split time with their dads. And you know Dez's situation." Strange how Nicanor could have an equally rough beginning and end up so differently than the Jennings boys. "At least you turned out a lot better than him." She waited to see if Nicanor's silence was just the pause before speaking.

His breathing changed, becoming shallower and shorter, but he didn't say a word.

"Except for the lock picking, I guess," she said to ease his tension. Picking a lock to help people wasn't in the same league as what Dez had done. "You do know it's illegal to do that here, right?"

He was quiet another moment. "You could have been hurt."

"Yeah." She knew what he had been thinking—suicide. She wished she could say the thought had never crossed her mind. But it was only a thought, one she immediately threw aside, feeling guilty she had even considered something so wrong. "They were just sleeping pills, by the way. And I only took one last night, as prescribed. I haven't been sleeping well."

"I understand." His tone said that he truly did.

At least with him, she didn't have to put on a pretense. She didn't have to fake she was better than she was, and she didn't feel as frustrated as with her family either. He hadn't tried to control her or even help once since she awoke. He was just there. The change made her feel like she could finally breathe.

With the breathing came her old craving for coffee. "Nicanor?"

"Yes."

Good, he was still sitting across from her. She couldn't be sure, since he was impossible to hear when he moved. "If you can't make coffee either, where are we going to get some?"

"We could ask Mrs. Peters."

Was he joking? She remembered the other time he had seemed to be teasing, and his face hadn't given a thing away. Now she thought she heard a small change, like a tiny note of humor in his voice.

"I don't think so." She wished she could smile, but the darkness pressing in and around her left no room for it. "Maybe I'll do it." She waited for him to protest or at least act surprised.

He did neither, not saying a word.

"Can you ... promise not to watch?"

He paused, then said, "If you wish."

Her heart didn't flip this time and there were no flutters in her stomach, but the words gave her the push she needed to stand and feel her way through the darkness to make the coffee.

Nicanor was silent as she fumbled through the task, and he was mostly quiet for the next hours he spent at the apartment.

The silence wasn't awkward, but peaceful, listening to his even breathing and knowing she didn't have to talk. Not talking was a strange thing for her. When a person was around, Oriana used to chatter nonstop, but her grim thoughts these days didn't lend themselves to small talk. The only problem with the silence was that it left her still alone with those thoughts. They gnawed on her, drawing her deeper into the hopeless pit she was in.

As Oriana sat on the sofa, Nicanor in the nearby armchair, she wanted to interrupt the silence and ask him more about himself. This might be her chance to unravel the mystery he still was to her, but she had probably already asked too much. She shouldn't risk scaring him away.

The apartment door opened. Oriana tilted her head toward the sound.

"Hello," her mom called out. "I've brought your dad along."

Oriana sighed. So much for not scaring Nicanor away.

"Hi, honey," her dad said, his voice getting closer to the sofa. "How are you feeling?"

She stifled a cringe at his question as she answered with the usual lie. "Fine."

"Good." He laid a warm hand on her shoulder, seemingly from behind her. He must be standing behind the sofa. "You look beautiful."

Oriana's cynical heart softened slightly at her dad's encouragement, and she put her hand on his. Even if he was stretching the truth, she appreciated that he seemed to believe his daughters were always beautiful. She suddenly remembered that Nicanor was sitting there, probably watching. "Dad, you remember Nicanor?"

"Of course."

He pulled away. Knowing her dad, he was probably going over to shake Nicanor's hand.

"Met you at the wedding, right?"

"Yes." Nicanor's voice was slightly deeper and more firm than before.

"So you're visiting Oriana. How long have you been here with her?"

Oriana had to stop herself from groaning. Was her dad actually going to do his protective papa routine?

"Since this morning." Nicanor's tone was still solid and confident. At least he wasn't intimidated.

"Marcus," her mom interrupted, before Oriana felt she had

to tell him this wasn't a date scenario. "Nye asked him to stay with Oriana until I got here. Don't you remember me saying? It was very sweet of you, Nicanor. Thank you."

Heat rushed to Oriana's cheeks. If only the sofa cushions would swallow her up so she could disappear. Welcome to another episode in the charity case of Oriana Sanders. Her mother's declaration was a painful reminder, but probably one she needed—Nicanor had only come as a favor to Nye, just putting in a good deed for the day.

"I'll leave, then. Mrs. Sanders, Mr. Sanders," he said as a farewell.

Oriana held her breath, wondering if he'd feel the need to acknowledge her now.

"Good-bye, Oriana." Her name sounded like a poem when he said it, lilting and delicate.

She desperately wanted to ask if he was going to come back, but she stopped herself. He had seen enough of the mess she was now. She shouldn't complete the humiliation by begging him to return for more. "Bye," she murmured.

As soon as the door closed, her mom started up again. "He certainly seems to be a nice young man now. I was never too sure about him, from what Nye told us and the tragedy with Dante."

"That was not his fault, Mother," Oriana snapped, flushing with anger at the insult to Nicanor's character.

The apartment fell deathly still.

Her dad cleared his throat. "No, Nye said it was an accident. I know she really seems to trust him now."

Oriana bit her tongue to avoid showing her parents more of her feelings for Nicanor than she already had. Where guys were concerned, her mom could get suspicious on much less evidence.

"He was very polite at the wedding. Quiet, but well-mannered." Her mother's voice came from farther away, probably the kitchen. "What did you two do the whole time he was here?"

"We just talked ... and sat."

"You should have him read to you the next time he's here. He has a lovely voice, the few times I've heard him actually speak. And that accent ... "

"You women and accents," Oriana's dad interjected, humor in his tone.

"It's not just any accent, dear. It took me some time to get used to your Texas drawl."

"Well, it's a good thing I lost it pretty quickly then."

If she had been in a better mood, Oriana would have smiled at her parents' banter.

"Would you like me to read to you, Oriana, or do you dislike my accent, too?" The cushion made a rubbing sound as her dad sat in the chair Nicanor had vacated.

"No, thanks," she answered, humorlessly.

"Are you sure? I see your Bible is on the table here. Have

you been able to keep up with reading it lately?"

"No, I haven't been able to read much lately, Dad." Her words dripped with sarcasm.

"I've offered to read the Bible to you," her mom called from the kitchen. "You said you prefer the magazines."

Oriana sighed, bracing herself for a lecture from her dad. Nothing came.

She knew he was watching her. At least she thought he was. Probably pointing one of those stern stares at her. If only he would just have the look of understanding that she had seen him give Nye in the past.

She thought she heard him get up from the chair.

He walked to the sofa, and the cushion beside her moved as he sat down. "Mind if I sit here?"

"I guess not."

He put a comforting arm behind her shoulders, and suddenly she was ten years old again, snuggling with her daddy, wanting to cry on his shoulder.

"He won't light your way until you want to see again, honey." Her dad's voice was low and soothing, but his words shot through her like a surge of electricity.

"Did you tell her about the wreath?" Her mom spoke from close behind the sofa, saving Oriana from having to react or think about what her father had just said.

"No."

"We found a wreath outside the building with your name

on it. We brought it in. Do you want it on the door?"

"A wreath?" Oriana wondered if she had heard correctly.

"A Christmas wreath. I was going to get you one myself, but I wasn't sure you'd want to decorate as much as you used to."

"The note didn't say who it was from," her dad inserted. "Just said, 'Miss Sanders.'"

"Maybe from one of your kids?" her mom suggested.

"They're not my kids anymore, Mother."

Another silence, shorter this time.

"I wish you could see the wreath," her mom said. "It has purple and green ornaments with silver threading through the whole thing. It's lovely, if a bit small. We could use those colors for the rest of your decorations."

Oriana leaned forward, away from her dad. "Why would I decorate?" She assumed the question would be taken rhetorically.

"Christmas is only fifteen days away." Of course, her mother answered anyway.

So soon. She hadn't kept track. In fact, she had forgotten about Christmas completely until now. Why would someone send her a wreath? She couldn't see it, and with or without it, Christmas would be just as black as every other day.

"Oriana, did you know those jeans have holes in them?" Disapproval was palpable in her mother's sudden question.

"I didn't know I was going to have company, Mother."

Funny how it took blindness to help Oriana understand why Nye had been so irritated with their mother for the past couple years. Without thinking, she was even saying "mother" instead of "mom," just like Nye. Her mom had never seemed so critical before, so overbearing.

Oriana stood, wanting to escape before she was so stifled she couldn't breathe. "I'm going to my room."

"What about lunch?" her mom asked.

"It's past lunchtime."

"You mean you ate already?"

"I mean I want to be left alone!" Oriana stumbled her way to the hallway, relieved to feel the smooth wall under her hands as she walked quickly to her room. She slammed the door behind her, not caring that she was acting like a ten-year-old. That's basically what she was now, that's how her family saw her and, inevitably, how Nicanor saw her. Poor blind little Oriana needed all the help she could get. Her father was wrong. She wanted to see more than anything. She wanted light. But there wasn't a trace of it in her pitch black world.

Jerusha Agen

Chapter Twelve

*"Oh, that I were as in the months of old,
as in the days when God watched over me,
when his lamp shone upon my head,
and by his light I walked through darkness ... "*
– Job 29:2-3

A thudding sound reached into the abyss where Oriana floated.

She slowly opened her eyes. A surge of panic, then a plunge into despair—the usual that came with waking to the darkness she forgot while she slept.

The noise came again. Someone knocking. Where was she? She felt what she guessed was the comforter of her bed beneath her hands as she pushed herself up. She must be in her room. "Who is it?"

"It's Dad."

Oriana relaxed at the sound of his voice. She must have fallen asleep when she escaped to her room. Not until after she had thrown a tantrum and snapped at her mother, she remembered with a twinge of shame.

"There's someone here to see you. Can you come out?"

Just what she needed—another gawker. "I'm pretty tired, Dad," she weakly called from the bed. "I think I'll just keep resting."

"It's a police officer."

Her heart beat sped up. Had they found Dez? Or James? "I'll be right there." She carefully slid off the bed and stood, trying to calm her breathing. Hopefully, the officer wouldn't need her to recount the whole attack again.

Giving her statement to the police after regaining consciousness had not been easy, especially since she was reeling from her blindness. She was unable to tell them anything clear the first couple days, but finally gave her statement to Officer Kelly. Something about the understanding patience of his approach put her at ease enough to be able to relive the attack and experience the humiliation of admitting she had been so stupid as to fall for the trap. Even so, the last thing she wanted was to go through that again.

She made her way to the door and opened it.

"He's in the living room." Her dad's voice was soft and close to her as she emerged from the room.

"How long did I sleep?"

"You were in there about an hour."

Oriana nodded and felt along the wall, hearing her dad follow behind her. Her mom's voice, talking to someone, came from the living room. Something jangled, like keys or maybe handcuffs, as Oriana approached.

"Miss Sanders. Officer Gabe Kelly."

"Yes?" Glad it was him, but she still held her breath until she heard why he was there.

"I just stopped by to see how you're doing."

"Oh." The tension seeped out of Oriana's body as a weary disappointment took its place. "There isn't any progress at all?"

"I'm afraid not, ma'am. We're watching James Jennings' usual hangouts, and we've got people trying to trace him. We're on the mother's home, too."

"Do you think you'll find them that way?" Oriana's dad asked.

There was a touch on Oriana's arm. "Come and sit down," her mom said quietly in her ear.

Oriana let herself be led to the sofa and guided into sitting while she listened to Officer Kelly's answer.

"I expect we'll find Dez Jennings eventually." Officer Kelly's voice directed toward Oriana still, as he must have turned to face her. "He's not savvy enough to evade us long-term, unless he sticks with his brother or the gang. This could have been his initiation into the gang, in which case he could be with them."

Oriana heard him sit in the chair opposite the sofa.

"I don't know if we'll get James. If he's smart, he's holed up somewhere, or he's left the city."

"Left?" Her mom interjected from next to Oriana. "You mean he might get away?"

"It's hard to say for sure, ma'am. Miss Sanders, I need to ask if there's anything else you can tell us about the younger brother. About his friends or where he might try to hide … where he goes for fun."

Oriana shook her head.

"Are you sure? From what I understand, you were pretty involved with him and his family. His mother says you visited her."

Oriana moistened her lips. "If you catch him, what will happen?"

Officer Kelly was quiet a moment, probably startled by her question. "Well, the case would go to court."

"Would he go to jail?"

"I can't really say. It would depend on the verdict, if they thought there was enough evidence to convict."

"Enough evidence?" A touch of anger laced her dad's voice. "They made her blind."

"Yes, I know that, sir." Officer Kelly sounded so calm. "But the Jennings' boys might have a lawyer who will try to claim insufficient evidence."

Her dad grunted with disgust.

"It helps that your friend saw the men leaving the scene, but his statement said he couldn't see them clearly in the dark, and that'll hurt."

They could go free. They might not be punished at all. The news sent a wave of nausea up Oriana's throat, leaving a bitter taste.

"Miss Sanders, is there anything else you can think of to tell me about the boy? You knew him well once."

She tried to remember what she knew, searching for the things they had talked about, the look on his face at church or when he defended her, but the effort was useless. All she could remember was the outline of his small figure as he watched his brother grab her and fling her into a wall.

Fury more intense than she had ever felt heated her blood. Was this hate? She had loved Dez and dedicated herself to helping him. She thought he had grown to care about her, to trust her. How could he turn around and want her hurt? Or did he want her dead?

"No." Oriana forced the word past the bile in her throat. "I never knew him." It was the awful, dark truth.

The unmarked police car slowly passed the apartment building another time. Tucked in the shadowed doorway of the abandoned warehouse across the street, Nicanor was sure he went unnoticed. Two of the teenagers who loitered by the stairs of the apartment building stared at the black car as it passed while the others made an effort to act cool and uninterested.

They weren't doing anything wrong at the moment, but Nicanor remembered that automatic nervous reaction too well. The fear of being caught for past guilt … or for nothing. The police were the enemy, and the people who hurt you were your friends. Though in the slums Nicanor had known, the police were not nearly so present as here. His city didn't have the funds, the manpower, or even the streets for police to drive on. These spoiled drug dealing kids and gangbangers had no idea what ghetto living really was.

The police car had gone by twice in the last hour. They seemed to have the same idea as Nicanor—to watch the apartment where Dez lived in case he or his brother returned. The brother likely hadn't lived with his family for years and probably had somewhere to stash Dez. The apartment was too obvious a place to look for them.

Nicanor turned out of the doorway and headed down the dark sidewalk. Since he moved into the neighborhood, he had spotted several of the corners used for drug dealing. They would be more likely places for Dez to turn up. If only Nicanor had been able to see the boy's brother or the other bangers more clearly that night, but they had darted away into the darkness when Nicanor shouted. He had been too worried about Oriana to follow them. He still knew who they were. He should have lied and told the police he could identify them, but he told the truth before he meant to. Perhaps the compulsive honesty was his reaction to needing to hide so many secrets, so much guilt.

He shoved his hands in his jacket pockets as he walked. Large snowflakes started to fall, sometimes hitting his face in wet dots. He wondered what Oriana was doing now. Probably in bed, if the hour was as late as he thought. Was she able to sleep? He hoped that nightmares were not the reason she had to take sleeping pills.

He had to find Dez and his brother soon. Or perhaps the police would. At least then Oriana would know they were behind bars, and they were paying for what they had done. He would spend every night roaming these streets if he had to. Every night until they were caught.

If only he had a way to get inside information. He could disappear in some ways, but most of the locals were not ready to trust him.

At the corner ahead, a man approached two hooded bangers.

Nicanor slowed and paused by a barred storefront window.

They spoke in voices Nicanor couldn't hear from this distance, then briefly clasped hands in a greeting that was perfect for disguising a handoff.

Nicanor went a few steps back to a darkened doorway to settle in for a long night of watching this corner. If it helped Oriana, the effort would be worth it.

He watched the drug dealers hanging out for an hour. Nothing happened but users buying drugs or pleading to get some. Who was he kidding? He had no chance of finding Dez this way either. He was just a boy—these bangers wouldn't want him around when they were doing business. A boy would be with his friends, kids more his own age, or he would want to if he couldn't.

Nicanor knew just where to find them.

Chapter Thirteen

*"And I will lead the blind in a way that they do not know,
in paths that they have not known
I will guide them.
I will turn the darkness before them into light,
the rough places into level ground.
These are the things I do,
and I do not forsake them."*
– Isaiah 42:16

"Well, your credentials certainly are impressive enough, Mr. Pessoa."

Nicanor watched Principal Stewart push his glasses up his large noise.

"I looked them over when Oriana wanted you to come here and teach." Principal Stewart leaned forward in his chair, putting his arms on the desk as if about to share a secret with Nicanor. "And I don't mind telling you, I've taken more than a few complaints from the teachers who have to sit with the detention kids since Oriana ... well, since the incident. I'm sure they would be relieved to have you take over the time, even if it is for dancing."

Nicanor, sitting in the chair on the other side of the desk, lifted an eyebrow.

"Not all of the teachers approve of Oriana having the kids learn to dance or really any of the things she had them do." He took a file folder from the top of the tall stack beside him. "Didn't she tell you?"

"No."

"Well, I guess she wouldn't. She was always so … positive." The principal gave Nicanor a small fake smile before opening the file and perusing the papers inside.

"Yes. She *is*," Nicanor countered, letting his irritation cloud his voice. Oriana wasn't dead.

Principal Stewart looked up. "Right. How is she doing, by the way?"

"She's blind." The obvious answer to a stupid question.

"Yes, of course." He seemed to only half understand. "We wanted to send flowers, but that didn't seem to make sense with … the way she is now. I'm sure she'll be delighted you're taking over her class. It was so important to her—really her main project here at the school. Tragic how it turned out. Just tragic."

He pushed his glasses up again. "I've had a terrible time getting the teachers to do anything with that group now, given what happened. They're downright scared to get near those kids. I can't say I blame them." He looked down at the file, then glanced up. "I don't mean to discourage you. You'd be doing us a great favor if you still want to take on the kids. You do seem like a man who could handle them and not be bothered by all the ... violence." His lips pushed up in a close-lipped half smile.

"I'll do it."

"Excellent." The principal stood and came around the desk to shake Nicanor's hand as he also rose from his chair. "The custodian unlocks the door before detention every day," he said quickly, as he led Nicanor to the door of the office, "so you just need to be here at three and keep the children busy for an hour. If you have any questions, don't hesitate to let me know. We'll expect you this afternoon then."

He pulled the door open just as a man wearing a baseball cap leaned into it.

The guy caught himself from falling and grinned at Nicanor. "Hey, didn't I see you with Oriana?"

Nicanor didn't respond. The man gave off jock vibes as strongly as some men smelled of cigars and leather.

"This is Nicanor Pessoa, Davis. He's going to take care of the afterschool kids." The principal gestured between them. "Nicanor, Davis Wentworth, our basketball coach and PE instructor."

"You're a teacher?" Davis looked Nicanor up and down, skepticism lacing his voice.

"Nicanor is a dance instructor, Davis," the principal answered.

Nicanor could have made good money predicting the amused smirk that slid onto Davis's face.

"Dancing, huh?"

Nicanor met the man's juvenile grin with an unflinching stare.

Davis sobered up and looked at Nicanor with challenge in his eyes. "Well, tap lessons aren't going to fix those kids." He grinned again, but it looked more like a sneer. "I bet Oriana knows that now."

Nicanor jerked toward Davis, ready to punch the smirk off his face.

"Hold it," Principal Steward barked. "Davis, that was uncalled for. Wait for me in my office." He easily slipped into his principal role as if dealing with two troublesome boys.

Davis stomped past Nicanor to go into the office.

Principal Stewart extended his hand to indicate that Nicanor should step outside, which he did as the principal followed and shut the door. "Davis has always had a … difficult personality. I apologize for his sense of humor, but I'm afraid I can't deal with two hotheads at once. I trust your reaction this time was an isolated incident."

Nicanor gave him a short nod. "It was." He couldn't afford to lose his chance at finding Dez.

"Good." The principal gave Nicanor a condescending pat on the shoulder and turned to go back into his office.

An inner-city school principal who couldn't handle a potential teacher conflict seemed ironic, but Nicanor knew he should be grateful. The principal's conflict avoidance may be the very thing that saved his spot at the school and his chance to help Oriana.

Oriana waved her hand in the vicinity of where she thought the shower faucet was, letting out a frustrated grunt when she still couldn't find it. Her knuckles whacked something hard.

Found it. Why couldn't she do anything without hurting herself?

She turned off the spraying water, and the chill of the air immediately hit her wet skin. She pulled the shower curtain aside and reached for the towel hanging on the rack. She couldn't feel it.

Fine. She stepped out of the shower only to catch her foot on the tub and tumble forward. She hit the hard vinyl floor with a smack. At least she landed on her arm and side instead of her head. She probably would have been paralyzed or something this time if she damaged her vulnerable head again.

Then again, maybe she *had* hurt her head. She felt disoriented, not sure which way she was facing anymore. Nervous swirling started up in her stomach as she slowly got to her knees, wincing at a sharp pain in her arm.

She swept her hand along the floor to her right, feeling nothing but the nobs and crevices of the vinyl. She tried the left, and her fingertips hit something solid. She moved closer to it. The toilet, she guessed. That meant the counter was just ahead to the left. She felt for the cabinets under the counter and breathed when her fingers found the corner edge. To think the bathroom had once been so calming, with the wall colors she had so carefully picked out and painted. Just a lot of wasted effort now.

She followed the cabinet up to the counter with her hand as she carefully stood, the wet floor slippery beneath her feet. Nothing like going for a crawl on the bathroom floor after getting cleaned up in the shower.

She hadn't showered for three days because the task was such a huge ordeal, but she thought the time had come to try again. A certain tango dancer might have had something to do with her motivation, though she knew she was being silly. He wouldn't even come back again.

A muffled ringing sound floated from somewhere.

Her phone. She had left it in her room. She thought.

Oriana trailed her fingers along the edge of the counter to reach the door where her robe should be hanging. She clutched the soft terry and felt for the armhole. Her arm hurt as she shoved it into the sleeve, but she ignored the pain and closed the robe around herself as best she could.

She felt for the doorknob with her still wet hand, the phone ringing outside. As quickly as she could, she found her way down the hall to her room. She reached the doorway, and the ringing stopped.

Rats. Probably went to voicemail.

She went into the room and found the chair where she had left the cell phone. She picked it up, hoping she could access her messages by feel.

She started when it rang and vibrated in her hand. Pushing what she hoped was the right button, she put the phone to her ear. "Hello?"

Breathing. A raspy sound, as if someone was intentionally breathing harder than normal.

"Hello?"

"Snitch once, you can't see. Snitch twice, you can't be," a voice whispered.

The phone fell from Oriana's hand. Or she let it go. She wasn't sure. Her hands shook as she dropped to her knees and felt the floor. She had to end the call, turn off the phone.

Her fingers touched the plastic of the phone. She picked it up.

Laughter. Cackling. The man was laughing on the other end. It had to be James.

Oriana trembled as she moved her thumb over the buttons, finding the one she thought would end the call. She pressed it hard. How would she know if it worked? The same button was supposed to turn the phone off. She held it down, holding her breath, heart pounding as she waited for the little jingle that always played as the phone shut down.

The tinkling sounded at last.

Oriana breathed, drawing shaky gasps as she sagged back to a sitting position on the floor.

A loud buzz made her jerk.

The door. Someone was downstairs. What if it was James?

She got up and stumbled toward the bedroom doorway. She walked quickly through the hall, running her fingertips along the wall. The wall ended. She stopped, her breathing shallow as she waited, listening.

A creak on the stairs. How could he get in? Mrs. Peters wouldn't have let him in, would she?

The footsteps stopped at the door.

He knocked, making her jump. She bit her lip. Could he pick locks as easily as Nicanor?

"Oriana?"

Nic. Oriana had never been so happy to hear a voice in her life. She quickly felt her way to the door and opened it. "Nicanor?"

"Yes."

She reached for him without thinking.

He didn't say a word, just took her into his strong arms and held her as she buried her face in his leather jacket. She didn't even care that it held a trace of cigarette smoke smell. She felt safe there in his embrace. If only it could last.

But it couldn't. She shouldn't be clinging to him like that. Embarrassment for the way she had thrown herself at him flushed her face, as she pulled away. At least she didn't have to see his expression, no doubt reflecting disgust or amusement. "I'm sorry," she murmured.

"What happened?"

She couldn't read anything from his even tone. "Nothing really." She must look crazy. Wet, mussed hair, and the robe she just remembered. She clenched the front of the collar together at the neck to be sure nothing showed. How humiliating. One little phone call was apparently enough to reduce her to spineless mush now. She shouldn't give a creep like James the satisfaction. He didn't deserve even that much from her.

"You were frightened."

"Yeah, sorry. I know I'm a mess." She tried to think of something to change the subject. She couldn't tell him about the call. He didn't need another reason to think she was helpless and vulnerable. "I wasn't expecting anyone." Hoping, but not expecting.

"Should I have called?"

"Called?" Her guilty, nervous mind jumped on the idea with a spark of fear. Did he know? Relax. She was just being paranoid. She forced herself to breathe. "Oh ... no. I'm just surprised you came back for more. I'm not exactly fun to be around these days. Did Nye make you promise you'd put in a certain number of days or something?"

"Do you not want me here?"

"No. I mean, yes," she answered quickly, despite noting that he ducked her question with one of his own again. "That's not it. I just don't want you to feel like you have to babysit me, that's all."

He was quiet a moment. "I wanted to come."

The heart she had declared dead warmed with longing to believe he meant that, but she had learned her lesson. Believing things that were too good to be true could explode in her face. She swallowed, searching for her voice. "I should go change. Do you mind?"

"No. I'll wait."

"Okay. Make yourself at home." She turned and felt her way back to the bathroom. How strange to picture Nic in her apartment, sitting on her sofa or waiting at the table. She tried to hurry as much as she could with blow-drying her hair and changing into the hole-free jeans and sweater set her mother had laid out the night before. By the end of the effort, she had two more bruises and one scratch but still took four times as long as she should have. She wouldn't be surprised if he had left already by the time she found her way back to the where the hall started.

"Nicanor?"

"I'm here."

He was close. Very close. Had he waited by the hallway the whole time? Trying not to show that his proximity affected her, she raised her hands away from her sides, as if showcasing the final result of her change. "All dry and warm, at least. I'm sorry, I probably got your jacket wet before." She blushed as she remembered how she had clung to him.

"It was wet already."

"Oh. Is it snowing?"

"Yes."

"I used to love the snow." She would never see snow again—the perfect beauty of an undisturbed blanket of white flakes, shimmering as the sunlight touched them. "I bet it's beautiful," she said, wistfully.

"I suppose it is." He sounded like he hadn't thought about it before.

She braved a couple free steps to pass him, immediately regretting going away from the wall. She felt around to her right, hoping he wasn't watching. "Is school cancelled?" The question came out naturally before she realized she had thought it. School cancellations were always her first consideration anytime there was a snowstorm. Old habits die hard.

"No."

"I'm not surprised. Our district hardly ever cancels. They did one day last school year when there was a real blizzard." She knew she was chattering, but maybe it would distract him from watching her as she tried to find the table and chairs. "I was stupid enough to drive in the blizzard anyway, but I still love—loved—a good snowstorm, even after the accident."

"Accident?"

Her fingers touched the back of a chair. She grabbed it, trying to keep relief from showing on her face. At least she hadn't hit her foot on it for once. "Um…" What were they talking about? Oh, the accident. "Yeah, a semi hit my car in a blizzard last year. The driver couldn't see me, the visibility was so bad. He slid across into my lane." She let go of the chair and reached for the edge of the counter, making contact with the cool marble after a few steps.

"Why were you driving?" His voice told her he was following, though at a distance.

That was probably his polite way of asking why she did something so stupid. "Timothy, a boy in the afterschool program that year, left his backpack at the school with his dad's phone in it. He was going to be in some pretty serious trouble if I didn't get it for him."

"So you risked your life to get it." He sounded like he was having a hard time understanding her reasoning.

"Yeah, pretty dumb, huh?" She followed the counter around to the kitchen side.

He paused, as usual, before he answered. "You love the children."

She stopped her search for the coffeemaker, feeling his words like another weight tied to her sinking heart. "I'm not sure I do. Now."

He was silent, but she could feel him watching. Was there judgment in his blue eyes?

"It really didn't do me much good." She didn't know why she felt the need to defend herself, but she kept going. "The doctors say that first accident, the coma I was in afterward, is probably part of the reason I'm blind now." She let out a sardonic chuckle. "Nye keeps reminding me that the doctors say it's a miracle I didn't have more severe brain damage or die with this second blow to my head. So, you are looking at a miracle." She pointed to herself with heavy sarcasm.

He still didn't say anything.

She let the silence drag on until she couldn't take it anymore. "I'm sorry. I told you I'm no barrel of laughs these days." A severe understatement, but the best she could do by way of apology for what she couldn't change. Even for Nic, she couldn't be happy. Not with this darkness swallowing her slowly, day by day.

"I don't need to laugh."

That seemed true enough. He never laughed anyway. Maybe he was the best person to be with her. Regardless, she couldn't ask him to spend half of his day there, doing nothing again.

"Come with me."

The sudden command startled her from her thoughts. "What?"

"I want to show you something." His voice was closer, like he had come to face her at the other side of the counter.

She moistened her lips. "I can't see, if you remember."

"You don't have to."

"I can't go outside." She had the distinct premonition that was what he had in mind.

"Yes. You can." His voice was firm—as if he was stating a fact as well as a command.

She opened her mouth to protest, then closed it. Despite her fear, despite the way her stomach clenched in horror at the thought of going out, some part of her was silly enough to wonder if he could be right.

"Will you come with me?"

Was this really Nic, the man of her schoolgirl dreams, asking her to go with him? His tone, if she believed what she heard, said that he truly wanted her to say yes. That he cared.

"Okay," she heard herself say.

"Good. Where is your coat?"

If she didn't know better, she'd say he sounded excited. Almost. "In the closet by the door." She came out from behind the counter, heading for the table while he went to get the coat. She heard the closet door open.

"The red?"

"Sure." At least he hadn't suggested the black coat—the one she had worn that night. She wondered if it had found its way back to her closet.

"Here." He was close to her again as she rounded the table. He gently put the coat in her hand. "I brought your boots."

At least he didn't hold the coat open to put it on her, or she never would have found it. She ran her fingers over the wool to locate the collar, surprised at how well she remembered her visual image of it. She slipped the coat on with relative ease, relieved since he was probably watching.

She bent and felt around for the boots, which suddenly met her hand. They were slip-ons, so even she could get into them without too much difficulty.

"Do you want socks?"

Her face got hot as she thought about him watching her shove her bare feet into the boots. How embarrassing. "No, I'm good." She tried to feign nonchalance by slipping her hands into her pockets but, no doubt, just looked clumsier when she had to fumble to find them.

"Ready?"

If he wasn't quite excited, she could tell from his voice that he was at least pleased. What was he planning? For some reason, she wasn't worried, though maybe she should be. "Yes, but ... " she swallowed, "you'll have to help me." The words stung in her throat. She hated having to say that, most of all to Nic.

"Thank you."

That was not the response she expected. "For what?"

"For the honor."

Was he for real or was she dreaming? No, she was blind and would never have a chance with the perfect guy—that had the bitter taste of real life. She reached out her hand anyway.

She soon found his arm, probably with help from him, and gently grasped just below his elbow, the way the nurses at the hospital had told her to do. Nic's warmth permeated the leather of his jacket under her fingers.

"Do you want your mittens?"

"Oh, yeah, I suppose so." Her brain was far too preoccupied to recall what she used to automatically think of when she went outside. How did he remember she wore mittens instead of gloves? "I think they're in my pocket." She reached with her left hand to grab the bunched up mittens from her coat, finding the pocket faster this time. At least the fact that they were mittens made them easier to put on the right way.

She found his arm again. "Okay. I'm ready." The flutter in her stomach denied the words. What if someone saw her out there? What if she fell? What if she lost her hold on Nic and got lost? She might never find her way back inside.

One by one, her fears dissipated as Nic led her as naturally as if he had been doing it his whole life. She may not be able to hear him move when he was farther away, but he was incredibly easy to follow up close. No stumbling or pulling the wrong direction like she had done when others tried to lead her.

She could feel where he was going to move before he went there.

In his calm, smooth voice, he warned her when they reached the steps and told her how many there were before going silent, trusting her to count on her own. She wanted to ask when he had figured out how many there were, but she was too busy making sure she didn't miscount and fall on her face.

She breathed again when they finally touched even ground and Nic told her there was a turn. She hoped Mrs. Peters wouldn't peek out of her apartment when they reached the bottom floor. An audience of one was more than enough.

Nic opened the outside door, and her breath left her in a gasp with the first smack of cold air that hit her face. She had forgotten what the air felt like, what it smelled like. The breath of winter was cold, but wonderfully fresh and clear. She followed Nic out the door, suddenly eager for more of the glorious change from her apartment. She hadn't realized how stuffy her rooms had become after two weeks of never going out, never even cracking a window.

Something wet touched her face, and she automatically swiped at it with her mittened hand. Then she realized what it could have been. "Is it still snowing?" As they continued to walk, she felt and heard the crunch of snow under her boots.

"Yes."

"Are they big, fluffy flakes?"

He didn't say anything for a moment, then, "Very big and

very fluffy."

"I wish I could see it," she whispered, the sadness of her dark reality closing in around her again.

"We can do better." He guided her to turn to the left.

"Where are we going?"

"A few more steps. We need to go to the other side of the bushes."

They must have been following the path out the door, lined with the bushes they were now going around. "Why?"

"Shh. You ask too many questions."

If she didn't know better, Oriana would say there was a note of teasing in his voice.

He stopped. "Wait here."

The anxious knot in her stomach reappeared as soon as he gently pulled his arm away. Where was he going? She couldn't be alone out here.

Stop it, she reprimanded herself. It was Nic. He wouldn't leave her.

"Hold out your hand."

She could have collapsed with relief at the sound of his warm voice, right in front of her. Trying to appear unruffled, she did as directed.

"Take off the mitten first."

"Why?"

He didn't answer.

Too many questions, she supposed. She obediently tugged

off the mitten and held out her hand again.

Something extremely cold plopped into her palm. The object was wet and freezing, but unbelievably soft, as if the slightest touch would crush it. "Is that snow?" Wonder filled the question as she felt the plushness and fragility of what must be a pile of snowflakes. She could feel the individual flakes as they touched her palm, her fingers, then melted into the soft cushion she carefully held.

"I don't think I've ever felt it without gloves before." She spoke quietly, as if talking loudly would make the snow melt faster. "It's so soft," she added with amazement. Before she knew it, her lips had shaped into a smile.

"Still beautiful." The emotion in his voice revealed that he, too, was feeling wonder.

"Yes … it is." The last of the snow melted into liquid in her hand. She hadn't noticed until then how chilled her skin was. Her hand almost hurt. She shook it to get some of the moisture off.

"Are you cold?"

"Yeah. I guess there's a reason I usually wear gloves."

Nic caught hold of her hand and cradled it between his, covering it in warmth. How did he stay so warm without even wearing a decent coat? The irrelevant question was all her fogged mind could think of with his hands around hers. She felt a definite spark, and it had nothing to do with static electricity this time.

"Better?"

"I—" She moistened her lips and tried again. "I think so." Could she honestly say that when her heart was setting a new world speed record?

He slowly lifted her hand and she forgot to breathe, wondering if he was really going to do what she thought.

He did. He kissed her hand like a knight in the movies. She thought she might swoon. Was he looking at her? She could only imagine how handsome and gallant he looked right now, his blue eyes on her. Like something out of her dreams.

He took the mitten from her other hand and slipped it on the one that was now warm as could be. He moved to stand beside her and put her hand on his arm so that she could follow his lead. She did so with something almost like hope, for when he kissed her hand, she believed she had seen a glimpse of light.

Chapter Fourteen

"Clouds and thick darkness are all around him; righteousness and justice are the foundation of his throne."
– Psalm 97:2

Nicanor tried to see with Oriana's eyes as he met the hostile stares of her students.

"Look who came back." Juan crossed his arms and leaned back with a grin while the other kids in the afterschool class laughed.

Nicanor felt quite the opposite of the compassion and love that Oriana had for these kids. They may be young, but they were already pitiful products of the streets. They were obviously prejudiced, with the Hispanics and Latinos grouped at one table and the blacks at another. Most of them smelled like cigarette smoke or marijuana and flashed more attitude than bangers. It was like staring at his twelve-year-old self.

"Ain't you scared of us?" The girl who Nicanor thought was called Jonique loudly snapped the gum she chewed.

"Should I be?" Nicanor met her gaze, prompting her to look away and mutter something under her breath.

"The other teachers are." A half-grin tilted Juan's mouth

as he picked up the challenge. "You know what happened to Miss Sanders."

"Shut up, Juan." The sharp scold came from LaTisha at the other table.

"Why?" Juan glared at her. "Mad 'cause your boyfriend's gonna get busted?"

"He's not my boyfriend." LaTisha dropped her gaze to the table in front of her. "He didn't mean to hurt her."

She said the last words quietly, but Nicanor caught them. He had found his lead to Dez, and, from the sounds of it, she had spoken to him since the attack.

A little hand went up at the back of the Hispanics' table.

Nicanor had forgotten about tiny Maria, hidden behind Juan. "Yes, Maria?"

She smiled shyly. "Are we gonna dance?" She shrank down into the chair, barely getting the question out.

"Yes."

"Aww, man. That stuff's for pansies." Juan tilted his chin and looked at Nicanor. "I ain't doing it."

"I believe Miss Sanders taught you better English, Juan."

"You don't talk perfect."

"I didn't grow up here."

"So what?"

"So … " Nicanor took a step toward the boy, looking at him directly. "Let's have a wager."

"What?" Juan's defiant glare faltered with his surprise.

"I'll bet that I can tell you what's in your pocket. If I win, I get to keep what is in there, and you have to dance with the other children."

"What if you lose?" The challenge came back into Juan's eyes.

"Then you don't have to join in the dance lessons." Nicanor glanced at the other students, who all stared at him as if he had just fallen out of a spaceship. He got the feeling Oriana had never used this technique before. "Do we have a deal?"

"Okay, sure. What's your guess?"

"Cigarettes."

Juan frowned.

"Is he right?" One of the kids asked, amid several similar questions thrown at Juan.

Juan reached into his pocket and slowly took out a smushed pack of cigarettes. He smacked it down on the table in front of him and glared at Nicanor.

"Look who's busted now." A boy at the other table snickered.

A glance at LaTisha told Nicanor he had just doubled his winnings—she now watched him with a big, satisfied grin on her face.

An hour later, Nicanor hoped to capitalize on the approval LaTisha showed him during the dance session, especially when he had singled her out to demonstrate a new move to the class.

"May I walk you out?" Nicanor asked the girl, as she slung her backpack over one shoulder.

She looked at him with her eyebrows raised. Then a smile with a hint of shyness appeared. "Sure, if you want to."

Nicanor grabbed his coat from the chair and walked with LaTisha, following the other departing kids who sprinted and sauntered down the dark hall to the stairs.

"How's Miss Sanders?"

Perfect. Nicanor hadn't been able to come up with a way to approach the topic of Dez, though he had thought about it in the back of his mind during the whole class. LaTisha just gave him his lead in. "Not good." Even in the dark, he could see LaTisha frown and drop her gaze.

"Does she hate us now?" Her voice trembled with the quiet, barely perceptible question.

"No ... She loves you." He could have made up the comforting answer, but he didn't have to. Oriana seemed to be trying to hate the kids, to be angry at them, but he knew a love like she had for them was not so easily killed. He let his words sink in until he and LaTisha reached the stairs and started down. "She would feel a lot better if she didn't have to be afraid."

"Miss Sanders is afraid?" The idea seemed unbelievable to LaTisha's young mind.

"Of course. The boys who made her blind are still out there, and they might do something to hurt her again."

She shook her head. "No, Dez wouldn't. He said it was an accident." She stopped and slapped a hand over her mouth, her eyes huge.

Nicanor paused on the stair below her and met her wide-eyed gaze. "You're friends with Dez?"

She slowly lowered her hand and nodded. Her gaze dropped to the floor.

"And you spoke to him."

She shrugged.

"LaTisha." Nicanor waited.

At length, she finally lifted her gaze to the general direction of his face.

"Miss Sanders can't see anymore because of what Dez and his brother did." He tilted his head in an effort to see her eyes. "They need to pay for that. We need to make sure they don't hurt her again. If you tell me where Dez is, I can do that."

She looked away again, shifting her weight as if she was thinking of escape.

"LaTisha, you can help me. You can help Miss Sanders. Please?" He could not believe he was pleading with a little kid, practically begging. The frustration would be worth it if she could lead him to Dez.

LaTisha was silent for a long, painful minute. Then she shook her head. "Last time I snitched, Miss Sanders got hurt. I ain't snitching again."

"LaTisha—"

She dashed around him and trotted down the stairs.

Nicanor watched her go, but he wasn't seeing her. He saw only Oriana's smile of wonder when she held the snow in her hand. It had left him awestruck—by her beauty and by how much he was starting to care. It made him want to run away like LaTisha. Maybe he was the coward his father always said he was. But he couldn't leave until he had done his best to bring that smile back again, until he set things right, even if that little girl just took his best chance of doing that with her.

※

A man stood in the shadows of the hallway by Nicanor's apartment.

Nicanor slowed his approach.

"Hi." The man stepped into the dim light that came from the bulb above him. Marcus Sanders.

Nicanor's heart rate continued at a faster pace, but he kept his expression calm. What was Oriana's father doing there? "Can I help you?" Nicanor stopped in front of Sanders. He wasn't about to ask him in to the pathetic one-room apartment.

"Marcus Sanders, Oriana's father. We met again at her place?"

Nicanor's terse response must have made Sanders think he hadn't been recognized. "Yes." Let him think what he wanted. "It's late."

"So I see." Sanders directed a pointed look at the whiskey

bottle that poked out of the paper bag in Nicanor's hand.

Perhaps Nicanor should have hid the evidence of his nightly ritual, but Sanders had that look in his eyes, the one Nicanor's father greeted him with every time Nicanor came home. The look that said it didn't matter what he did—he would never get approval.

"I need to talk to you about Oriana."

Nicanor waited.

"Mind if I come in?" He gestured to the apartment door.

Setting his jaw, Nicanor went to the unlocked door and pushed it open, leaving it ajar behind him for Sanders to follow.

Nicanor set the bottle on the counter and crossed his arms over his chest, watching Sanders' disapproval evolve into something close to disgust as he took in the surroundings.

He made an attempt to hide his reaction as he turned to face Nicanor. "I want to thank you, for what you did for Oriana that night when … " His voice choked with emotion that seemed to surprise Sanders as much as it disturbed Nicanor.

"It isn't necessary." Nicanor uncrossed his arms and braced one hand against the counter.

Sanders cleared his throat. "It is necessary. What you did wasn't. I'm very grateful." He took a few nervous steps in the direction of the mattress. His stared at it for a minute while Nicanor waited. A compulsory thank you couldn't be the only reason Oriana's father was here.

"That's what makes this so difficult." Sanders finally looked up and turned to Nicanor, as if needing to force himself. "I understand that Nye asked you to visit Oriana, and that's probably why you were there. But I know you've gone back since then, and I'd like to know what your intentions are."

Nicanor stared. He should have expected something like this, but he had never been in a relationship long enough to have to deal with a father. Not that he was in a relationship now either. Oriana's father misunderstood. Nicanor thought about his answer. He had better choose his words carefully. "I would like to help."

"Is that all? Just help the blind girl?"

Nicanor straightened as a pulse of anger coursed through his veins. Was this some kind of test? Or was Oriana's father really that much of a jerk? "I don't see her that way."

"Okay." Sanders took a few steps closer to Nicanor. "How do you see her?"

"I'm not sure what you're getting at." Nicanor met Sanders' stare head-on as he lied, refusing to squirm, if that's what the man wanted.

"I know you're Nye's friend, and she trusts you, but *I* don't know you very well." He cast a glance around the apartment, his gaze coming back to rest on the whiskey bottle. "And I don't much like what I see."

Nicanor's surge of temper burned hotter at the judgment. "What do you want?"

"I want you to stop seeing my daughter."

The flare of anger went out as if doused with ice water. Stop seeing her? Her little smile, the hint of light, perhaps even hope in her unseeing eyes, filled Nicanor's vision and grabbed at his heart.

"Oriana, I mean," Sanders clarified, unnecessarily. "She's vulnerable right now. I don't know how you feel, but I know my daughter, and I can tell she's starting to …" His gaze flitted about like he was trying to avoid admitting something. "She's starting to feel something for you. If you don't return her feelings, then she'll get hurt. And if you do," his wandering gaze landed on Nicanor again, "I'm afraid you'll both get hurt."

Nicanor clenched his jaw. "Why is that?" he forced out, telling himself he was just humoring the man.

"She's not herself right now. If she were …" Sanders again looked like he was uncomfortable with what he wanted to say.

"She wouldn't like a man like me."

Sanders nodded. "I mean no offense, but you don't share her beliefs. Oriana's Christian faith is the most important thing in her life. She would never intentionally get attached to someone who didn't share that."

"Or you don't want her to." Even as the words left his mouth, Nicanor didn't know why he felt the need to argue.

"That, too." Sanders met Nicanor's stare with a steady gaze.

The man was only doing what fathers were supposed to. Nicanor should be glad Oriana had a father who cared so much. She would be protected. From people like Nicanor. From Nicanor himself. The whole thing was ridiculous anyway. He didn't even care for Oriana, at least not in the way her father was thinking.

An unpleasant taste rose in Nicanor's throat, whether from defeat or frustration, he couldn't be sure. "You have nothing to worry about. I'm helping Oriana as a favor to Nye … and because I … think of Oriana as a friend," he added, not wanting to prove Sanders right about the "blind girl" remark. "That's all."

Nicanor's cell phone vibrated loudly on the counter. He had never been so pleased to get a call. "I have to answer this." He reached for the phone.

"Of course. I'm truly sorry if I've offended you. I am grateful, as I said."

"You must protect your children," Nicanor said dismissively, as he pretended to stare intently at the screen on his phone.

"Thank you." Sanders turned and went out the door.

Nicanor held the phone as it stopped ringing and waited for the vibration that would signal a voicemail message. He didn't usually listen to it right away, but this time he needed something to keep him from thinking about what had just happened.

The voicemail came through, and he held the phone to his ear to hear Terry's latest tirade.

"Nicanor, I have good news and bad." The agent's voice was strangely calm. "I wouldn't want to tell you this kind of thing over the phone, but you don't leave me any other choice. I just received word that your father has died."

Nicanor stopped breathing.

"He was found at his apartment by a friend."

His father didn't have friends.

"It seems they only had my contact info to reach you. The good news is he left a little money, and it'll cover your fees. Well, not entirely, but I'm willing to call it even. They sent details about the funeral. Call me if you want them."

Nicanor's breathing renewed, as if it had only stopped in fear of what else Terry might say. His father was dead. He felt nothing. Carlos Pessoa had been dead to him for twenty-three years. Dead since the day his mother died and Nicanor lived.

Nicanor looked at the empty darkness by the door where Sanders had just stood. Why didn't God give him a father like that? Sanders loved his children. He protected them.

Nicanor shouldn't be bothered so much that Sanders wanted to keep Oriana safe. Nicanor knew himself that he couldn't let anything happen between them. He would only cause her more pain. Her father was right. Nicanor should stay away from her.

Keeping his distance should be simple enough to do, since he only cared for her as the little sister of his friend. There was an unpleasant ache in his heart. Was he now lying to himself, as well?

Nicanor stalked away from the counter, wishing there was another mirror he could smash. He should stay away from her, but could he? The surge in his chest when he pictured her face was not the answer he hoped for.

Chapter Fifteen

*"I am the Lord; I have called you in righteousness;
I will take you by the hand and keep you;
I will give you as a covenant for the people,
a light for the nations,
to open the eyes that are blind,
to bring out the prisoners from the dungeon,
from the prison those who sit in darkness."*
– Isaiah 42:6-7

Oriana wanted to get out of bed. This morning was the first time since she had awoken blind that she felt that way. *Don't get your hopes up*, she cautioned herself. Hand kissing could be a daily ritual between casual acquaintances or even siblings in Argentina, for all she knew. Still, Nic's thoughtfulness, his gentleness as he persuaded her to go outside and showed her a new way to love a thing she thought she had lost—that had to mean something … didn't it?

The back-and-forth battle had waged in her mind as she showered, managing to stay on her feet and get dressed in record time. She didn't know how early Nic would come, and she wanted to be ready. It might be a Saturday, which could mean he would arrive later. If he still came.

She mentally shoved the pessimistic thought aside as she left the bathroom.

Someone knocked on the apartment door.

Oriana hurriedly felt her way to the door and swung it open with a smile.

"Well, honey, don't you look happy today?" Mrs. Peters exclaimed.

Oriana's lips sagged into a frown. "Mrs. Peters. I ... was expecting someone else."

"That nice young man with the accent, I bet." Her voice was rich with approval. "Well, I won't keep you. I just wanted to give you the gift your student dropped off."

"Gift?"

"Yes, I saw a boy leaving a shopping bag outside the door to the building. I asked him what he was doing and then when I saw he had 'Miss Sanders' written on a note on the bag, I said I would give it to you for him. He didn't want to come up himself."

Oriana's stomach clenched. "Did he give you his name?"

"No, but he said he was in your class."

"What did he look like?"

"Small and wiry. Black. He had on one of those bandanas or whatever they are under his cap. And those awful slacks that are too big—looked like they were going to fall down right in front of me."

Oriana swallowed as the details lined up. "What color was his jacket?"

"Well, let's see now … I think it was blue. Yes, a bright sort of blue."

Dez. The knot in Oriana's gut came back. "Thanks," she said automatically, as she started to close the door.

"Don't you want the gift?"

No, she didn't, but refusing to take it would just mean more questions and answers she didn't want to give. "Can you just set it inside the door, please?"

"Sure. I think it's a little Christmas tree. Looks decorated already." The bag rustled as Mrs. Peters set it down. "I've got some cookies in the oven, so I best get going."

"Okay." Oriana shut the door. So now her attackers were at her apartment. Should she report it to the police? There probably wouldn't be any point. They couldn't keep officers at the apartment for however long it would be until James and Dez were finally caught, if that ever happened. Dez wouldn't be stupid enough to keep coming back anyway. This delivery must have been a one-time stunt.

Unless that was the point, to kill her off with whatever was in the bag. The tree might be some sort of joke or cover for whatever they had really left her.

Oriana listened for a moment. She couldn't hear anything. Didn't bombs always tick? Or was that only in the movies?

She forced herself to let out the breath she held. She was

being silly. Where would Dez or James get a bomb? Guns or knives were more their style.

She shuddered.

The buzzer sounded, making her start. She felt her way to the speaker by the door. "Who is it?" She was suddenly security conscience, realizing how foolish she had been to just open the door with Mrs. Peters. The knocker could've been anyone.

"Nicanor."

She felt like crying at the sound of his voice. She pressed the button to let him in and waited by the door, trying to calm down and get ahold of herself. For once, she wanted to show him that she could actually be a rational, controlled person.

By the time she heard the telltale creak on the stairs, she was breathing normally and wore a pleasant, calm expression on her face … she hoped. She opened the door before he had to knock.

"Hi." Her lips pulled up into a small smile, as if of their own accord.

"Hi."

She thought he just stood in the doorway, even though she backed up a few steps so he could enter. She could feel his eyes on her. If only she could see him. She cleared her throat. "Thank you. For what you did yesterday."

He was quiet for a moment. "It was nothing."

"It was a lot. You gave me one thing back."

"I'm glad."

A muffled ringing sound came from somewhere down the hallway.

Oriana didn't move, not wanting to spoil the moment.

"Is that your phone?"

"I suppose so. I think I left it in my room." She turned and ran her fingers along the wall as she headed for her bedroom.

Another ring, much closer than she thought.

"Bathroom," she muttered to herself, as she turned into that room instead. She felt for the counter and found her phone as it rang again. "Hello?"

"Snitch once, you can't see."

Oriana's heart pounded at the voice, this time low-pitched and raspy.

"Snitch twice, you can't be."

Her hand shook, but she held on to the phone. "Who—" Her voice caught on her fear. "Who is this?"

"Snitch once, you can't see," he repeated in her ear.

"James?" she whispered.

He laughed.

"Oriana?" Nic spoke from the doorway. "Who is it?"

She held out the phone to him, her hand trembling.

He took it.

She could hear the loud cackling even from that distance.

"Who is this?" Nic's sharp tone sliced through the air.

The laughter stopped.

There was no sound. What was happening? Panic started to close Oriana's throat, making it hard to breathe. "Nic?"

"He hung up. What did he say to you?"

She shook her head. She was trying to forget it.

"Oriana, I need to know. What did he say?"

"Something ... " She swallowed, still not getting enough air. "Something about me being blind because I snitched ... "

"What else?"

She turned sideways and gripped the edge of the counter. "That something will happen to me if I snitch again."

He swore and made a smacking noise, as if he'd hit the wall or the door.

She could hear him walk this time, as he stalked down the hallway. "Where are you going?" She followed as quickly as she could.

"You know who that is. I'm going to the police. Then I'll find him and end this."

"Nic, no. They can't do anything. It was just a phone call. You might make things worse." At this point, she didn't know what scared her more—the phone call or Nic leaving her alone. "Please ... " She tried to catch her breath. Why couldn't she breathe? "Please, don't leave me," she gasped out.

He stopped moving.

She reached out a hand, which she was sure still shook like crazy.

He gently took her hand in his. "If you wish."

Before she knew it, she had gone into his arms, learning to breathe in the embrace of the only person who could make her feel this terrifying life was still worth living.

He was going to kill that kid.

Nicanor jogged across the dark, wet street as the rapidly falling snow coated his head and jacket. He didn't bother to glare at the punks who seemed to permanently live at the bottom of the stairs to the apartment building, even so late at night. He had only one thing on his mind.

He yanked open the creaking door and stalked down the long, stinking hallway. He barely heard the man and woman yelling from one of the apartments and only glanced at the old wino who staggered as he chugged his bottle.

Nicanor rounded the corner and was greeted by smoke from a teenager who leaned against the wall, getting his fix. Satisfied that the kid was too out of it to interfere, Nicanor rapped on the door to apartment twelve. He waited, listening to the baby's screams and fighting kids.

The door eventually opened a crack. "Shut up!" a woman yelled from the other side of it.

The children's noise quieted only slightly as she opened the door farther.

Dez's mother.

"Who are you?" Her voice was a smoker's sandpaper

scratch.

Nicanor couldn't stop the furious glare he leveled at her.

She started to close the door.

He kicked out his foot, stopping the door. "Where are they?" His fight was not with her, he reminded himself, trying to calm down before he did something he might regret.

Her eyes narrowed as she watched him through the crack of the door. "I know you. You was with my boy's teacher."

"Then you know she's not his teacher anymore."

Her gaze dropped.

"Where is he?"

She muttered something.

"What?" he bit out.

She looked up. "I don't know."

"You're lying."

"I wish I was." She met his gaze with one so steady he feared she was telling the truth.

Another dead end was not an option. The taste of the injustice rose in his throat as he stared at the worn down, pitiful woman. He hated her. He hated the whole worthless family.

He stepped close to her face. "I'll find them. When I do, you'll wish the police found them first."

Her eyes widened. Finally. She didn't look so tough now.

He turned to leave.

"Wait."

He glanced over his shoulder but didn't turn back.

She had the door open wider. "Please. Don't hurt 'em. Even if they done bad, they still my boys."

Nicanor walked away. Only a mother could love sons like them.

Only his mother had loved him.

He saw her face as he retraced his steps. Her blonde hair, her laughing blue eyes. He reached the door to the outside and pushed into it, only to have it jerked open so suddenly he had to catch himself from falling. He turned to see who the joker was and found himself staring at one of the most intimidating men he had seen.

The guy held the door open and watched Nicanor with a cheeky grin, looking like a cross between the The Rock from WWF and some U.S. football player Nicanor couldn't remember the name of—Terry's favorite sports heroes that he talked about far too much. If not for the police emblem on the burly man's jacket, Nicanor might have been tempted to run.

"Hey there." His rumbling voice fit his physique. "Nicanor Pessoa, right?"

Nicanor took a step away so the officer could let the door swing shut. "Yes," Nicanor answered, not at all comfortable with the huge man knowing his name.

"Officer Gabriel Kelly." He stuck out his hand. "Call me Gabe."

Nicanor looked from the hand up to his face. "What do you want?" Uneasiness stirred in his stomach. He never could trust the police, especially when they knew too much and wanted something from him.

Kelly lowered his hand, his smile fading. "You're the friend who stopped the attack on Oriana Sanders, right?"

"Have you been spying on her?"

The giant officer laughed. "No, nothing like that, though we have been running the patrols by there more often at night. You gave us a statement after the incident, remember?"

"I didn't see you, and they didn't take my picture."

"True enough, but we asked her sister who we should watch for at Oriana's place and who was okay the last time she called us, which is pretty often," he added with a grin. "You're one of the good guys, so we're okay." He sobered again. "But it's not okay for you to start taking matters into your own hands."

Nicanor just watched him.

Kelly nodded toward the apartment entrance. "I know you were visiting the Jennings in there. I can understand your feelings, Mr. Pessoa, but you have got to let us do our job. Don't do anything rash like try to get those boys yourself. We'll be able to find them and get a clean bust only if you don't jump in there and mess things up."

Nicanor avoided Kelly's gaze, which wasn't difficult given his greater height. Calming down a bit, Nicanor had to admit to himself that the officer might have a point. What would he have done if he had found Dez in the apartment when he stormed in? He wasn't sure he wanted to know.

"We want to arrest the bad guys, not the good ones, you know?" Kelly tried again. "So do we have a deal?"

Nicanor looked up. "I'll let you do your job. As long as you do it soon."

Kelly nodded. "Good enough for now. Have a good night, Mr. Pessoa." He touched the bill of his police cap with a slight farewell tilt of his head.

Nicanor breathed more easily as the big man walked to his police car on the street. Only a few minutes after he drove off, the smokers and druggies came out of hiding and congregated around the building again. Nicanor wondered why Kelly was so sure that Nicanor would keep his word—he didn't even stay to make sure Nicanor left. The man was either playing the odds or was just that naïve. Oriana was living proof that naïve wasn't safe in this world.

Jerusha Agen

Chapter Sixteen

*"But when I hoped for good, evil came,
and when I waited for light, darkness came."*
– Job 30:26

"But, honey, you haven't been to church in weeks."

Oriana held the phone away from her ear as her mom's loud exclamation came through.

"Don't you think you should go? Just say the word, and your father and I will swing by in ten minutes. We're just going to get in the car now."

"The word is 'no,' Mother." Oriana felt for the sofa cushion behind her and slowly sat down, pleased with her perfect aim.

"Honey, I have to tell you we're getting worried about you. It's not like you at all to want to miss church." The sound of worried tears gathered like a cloud over her mom's voice. "Why don't you want to worship anymore? Why aren't you reading your Bible? Can you tell me what's going on?"

Oriana swallowed, her conscience twinging under the direct onslaught of questions. The truth was, she couldn't tell her mom what was going on. She didn't understand it fully herself, and she knew her mother wouldn't like what she might say. "I just ... " She searched for something that was at least somewhat honest. "I'm really not comfortable in public yet." There, that was true. "I hate the thought of people seeing me like this." Very true. "Maybe when I figure out how to get around better and take care of myself more, then I can try it. It's just a lot to handle right now, okay, Mom?"

"Okay, sweetie. I'm sorry if I pressured you."

Oriana stifled a relieved sigh. "It's okay."

The buzzer sounded.

"Can you hang on a second? Someone's at the door."

"Sure."

Oriana got up from the sofa and took an embarrassing amount of time to find the intercom by the door—embarrassing because the voice on the other end was Nic's.

She put the phone to her ear as soon as she had buzzed him in. "Mom? I have to go. Nic's here."

"Nicanor? Good. Maybe he'll read some passages to you so you can at least have some worship time."

"Somehow I don't think he'd go for that."

"You've always had such a strong faith, Oriana. Don't let anything take that away."

Good advice, but what if it came too late? Oriana couldn't believe the thought even as it flitted through her mind. Is that really where she was at? She didn't know. She was so confused. "Okay, Mom," she managed.

She heard the door open.

"Is that him again?" Tension edged Nic's voice.

"No." Oriana shook her head. "It's my mom."

"Are you talking to Nicanor?" Caroline asked.

"Yeah, Mom. I have to go now."

"Okay, we have to get going, too. Why don't you just ask him? He might enjoy reading to you."

"Not the Bible, Mom."

"A few weeks ago, you would have jumped at the chance to get him to read you the Word."

The observation hit exactly where her mom had aimed—the target of Oriana's conscience. She was right. The old Oriana would have seen this opportunity a long time ago and pounced on the chance to reach Nic with the Gospel. Losing sight of God and not knowing where to find Him apparently worked like an extinguisher for her evangelistic fire.

Oriana sighed under the added weight of guilt. "Okay. I'll ask him. Have a good worship service."

"Bye, sweetie." She hung up before Oriana could say good-bye. Funny how quickly her mom was ready to end the conversation once she knew she had won.

"Ask me what?" Nic stood closer than she had thought.

So, there was some curiosity hidden beneath that implacable exterior Oriana remembered. "It's Sunday morning, and my mom wanted me to go to church. Like I used to," she quickly added, realizing she might be giving the impression of a reluctant churchgoer. "I haven't been there since, well, you know."

"Do you want me to take you?"

"Oh … no. She wanted me to ask you. That is … " She stopped. She sounded like a ten-year-old again. "Whenever I had to miss church before, getting sick or whatever, I would read my Bible and sing some hymns at home. Kind of like having my own worship time."

"You want to sing."

Was he joking again? "No, no. I was just going to ask you if you'd be willing to read some Scripture to me."

"Scripture? Is that different than your Bible?"

"No, sorry." She'd have to tone down the Christianese. Maybe he was less churched than she thought. "I just mean the Bible. I'm not sure where it is."

"On the coffee table."

The speed of his answer made her wonder if he had looked at it before. "Would you read some?" She still wasn't ready to hear Scripture herself, but she didn't want her own issues to keep him from finding help there, maybe even his salvation.

"If you wish."

She made her way over to the sofa and stubbed her toe on the armchair before she reached it. "Were you watching that?"

He paused before he answered. "Yes."

At least he was honest. Somehow, she didn't mind as

much anymore if he saw her klutziness. It hadn't driven him away so far.

    She sat on the couch and waited for him to sit on the chair. Instead, the cushion next to her dipped as he sat down. Her face heated as she sensed his proximity. Wow, she was still such a silly schoolgirl. The Bible was probably just right in front of him on the table, and that's why he sat there. Still, she was glad she had gone through all the poorly aimed sprays to put on perfume today. If only she could figure out how to do makeup.

    "Which part should I read?"

    "There should be a ribbon in there where I was reading last." A lifetime ago.

    "It's in Romans."

    Of course. The horribly overused Romans 8:28 and everything. Despite that passage being just about the last one she'd like to hear right now, she knew there was nothing like Romans for laying out the Gospel message. "That'll be fine. Why don't you start at the beginning of Romans?"

    He flipped some pages and began. He was a wonderful reader, easy to listen to, even if the words he read were not what she wanted to hear. Most of them were so familiar that her mind easily wandered onto pleasant things, savoring the smooth, even tones of Nic's voice as he spoke with his beautiful accent. Before she knew it, he had read a great deal more than she had expected and was halfway through the book, smack-dab in Romans 8.

"And we know that in all things God works for the good of those who love him, who have been called according to his purpose." He stopped. "There it is. The verse you didn't like to hear."

She opened her mouth to respond, but he continued to read before she could. He had gotten her attention back on the words now, and she heard the following verses loud and clear.

"If God is for us, who can be against us?"

That's what she had thought—what she believed with all her heart. Why wasn't God's protection enough?

"Who shall separate us from the love of Christ? Shall trouble or hardship or persecution or famine or nakedness or danger or sword?" Nic stopped. "You have words highlighted here."

She closed her eyes. "Yes. 'For I am convinced that neither death nor life, neither angels nor demons, neither the present nor the future, nor any powers, neither height nor depth, nor anything else in all creation, will be able to separate us from the love of God that is in Christ Jesus our Lord.'"

He was quiet a moment. "Impressive."

"Not really. A lot of Christians know that verse by memory."

He picked up with the reading again, but Oriana didn't hear him. She was lost in her thoughts, ruminating on the change in her life, in her heart. How was it that she was separated from the love of God, despite what He promised in

His Word? She couldn't feel His love anymore. She couldn't see Him or hear Him. She was lost in this dark world He had put her in, and He wasn't there to lead her out or show her the way.

"Do you believe that?"

The question startled Oriana out of her thoughts. "What?"

"That 'Anyone who trusts in him will never be put to shame.' Does that mean anyone who trusts in Jesus?"

"Yes."

"It says that 'Everyone who calls on the name of the Lord will be saved' and that 'It is God who' … How was it?" he flipped a page, "'justifies' and Jesus is the one who 'intercedes.'"

"Right."

"Just for the people He chose."

"Yeah. It can be confusing. You don't have to keep reading anymore." Oriana had heard quite enough.

"That word, 'justifies'—it means to make things right?"

"Yes." She should be thrilled with how intrigued he sounded, but her own inner battle was ruining the moment.

"Is that like forgiveness?"

"It comes with forgiveness. From the 'wages of sin,'" she added, dredging up her rusty witnessing skills.

"And this is what you believe?"

"It is." She answered automatically, but truthfully.

"It's too good to be true. Too easy."

"I know what you mean."

"The things I've done are too …" He drew in a shaky breath. "Too unforgivable."

Her heart cracked at the pain in his voice. She reached over to him, miraculously finding his hand without too much searching. "God can forgive anything, Nic. And I can't imagine that you would have done something so awful as you make it sound. You're a good man."

"No." He pulled his hand away.

"I know about your life before. Nye told me. You've been with other women, I know, but that was a long time ago. You're different now. You're with me." She wondered if he would contradict her, or if he would express what was blossoming in her own heart. That he cared for her as she had come to care for him. That—dare she think it?—they might be growing to love each other.

"I was by my phone when you called."

That was not the response she was hoping for. "What?"

"That night, the night you went to meet the boy. I heard it ring, but I didn't answer. I just sat there." He spewed out the words quickly, as if ripping off the bandage would hurt less.

"Did you know it was me?" She held her breath for his answer.

"No."

She let out the air. She knew he couldn't have done that to her. Even if he had, he wouldn't have known the call was serious. "You never could have known what would happen. You didn't even know why I was calling. You'll have to do better than that if you want to be unforgivable." She couldn't believe she actually felt spirited enough to tease, but the lightheartedness came out of great relief—he had scared her with his ominous pronouncement of guilt.

His arm brushed her sleeve as he moved. She heard what sounded like the Bible being closed and set on the table.

Her heart rate sped up as she became aware of how close he had ended up, the cushions having sunk toward each other during the reading. She felt him turn slightly toward her.

He was watching her.

She forgot to breathe.

He took her hand in his and lifted it. Her fingers were suddenly touching his face as he guided them to what felt like his temple. The scar. She gently traced the slight ridge under her finger.

"Do you know what that is?" He let go of her hand, and she lowered it away from his face.

"A scar?"

"It's the mark of a murderer. Oriana, I am a murderer."

She blinked. She opened her mouth, then closed it, not sure what to think let alone say.

"I killed Dante."

This was about Dante? "That was an accident, a boating accident. Nye said so."

"She doesn't know." He abruptly stood. "The boat was mine. I made him go with me though there was a terrible storm."

She could tell from his voice that he was pacing back and forth. "I know, Nic. It was just a mistake. He chose to go with you. Nobody made him do it."

"No. He knew I was going to take her out with or without him. He went because … he knew I wouldn't make it if I went alone."

"Wouldn't make it?" She tried to follow the pattern of his movement with her head.

He suddenly stopped walking. "I was high."

"High." Parroting was about all she could manage as she fought to believe he meant something different than what she was thinking.

"Drugs, Oriana. Cocaine."

"Cocaine."

"In Argentina, it is worse than your city. I started on marijuana when I was eight, paco when I was sixteen. Coke I didn't start until New York. Easy to get there, and I had money."

The darkness closed in around her, pushing, crushing, like those first days when she awoke to the blackness. It couldn't be true. He could not be like Dez and James. He could not be worse.

"Dante knew I was high, that I had more coke with me. He

was afraid I would kill myself. He knew I wanted to." Nic stopped walking again, and she heard him sit in the armchair.

"When he fell into the water in the storm, I ... I laughed." His words were squeezed, anguished. "I was so high, I didn't know what was happening. I hit my head on the rail or somewhere. I saw him floating away on the waves when I passed out. I still see him." Nic's voice dropped with the last words. "I killed him," he finished in a whisper.

Oriana thought she had known despair before. This was worse. How could she have so stupidly misjudged him? How could she have given her heart away to a drug addict, to the man who killed her sister's fiancé? He couldn't be prosecuted for it, but he was right, he was responsible for what happened—for Nye's agony for three years, for the pain of the whole family as they tried to comfort her and never could. He killed Dante and almost killed Nye, too.

The memory of her sister's agony deepened the darkness pressing in on Oriana. What would this do to Nye if she found out? Would it ruin her newfound happiness? What would she think if she knew Oriana had fallen for the man who had really killed her fiancé, more truly than Nye had ever known?

"Please. Say something."

How ironic. The stoic, silent Nicanor was asking her to speak. How dare he? How dare he waltz into their lives and act like a saint when he was actually harboring this secret, keeping this truth from all of them, while he pretended to care about them? About her. What was he really doing here this whole time? Did he really think that nursing Nye's blind kid sister would pay for what he had done? Bitter nausea rose in her throat. "Get out."

"Oriana, I'm sorry. Please. You will never know how sorry. I live in the shadow of his death, what I did, every minute."

"Tell it to Nye," she spit out. For the first time, she was glad she was blind—she didn't have to see his face. "Better yet, don't go near her." Oriana slowly stood. "Leave all of us alone. Go back to New York or wherever you came from. I never want to hear from you again."

He was quiet for what felt like a minute. When he spoke, she could tell he was standing about five feet away. "Then God can't forgive everything."

She clenched her jaw, refusing to allow him to prick her conscience. "Maybe He can. But I can't."

A moment later, the door to the apartment quietly shut.

Oriana stumbled toward the armchair. Her leg struck it, and she went down, landing on her knees. She gripped the arm of the chair and pressed her forehead against the rough upholstery as tears streamed down her cheeks. What happened to God's promises? There wasn't a trace of light, not a hint of His love in this cavernous pit of darkness.

Nicanor slammed through the door of Oriana's apartment building, trying to escape the walls that closed in around him. He stopped outside the door and bent over, heaving in the cold air. The bottom of his world had just been kicked out, and he was free-falling.

He had told himself he couldn't make up for what he had done, that no one should forgive him, that he deserved their hate. That justice should be done.

He never knew it would feel like being gutted out with a knife.

He closed his eyes, but he could still see the hatred in Oriana's stare when she told him to get out. Why had he expected anything different? He should be relieved, the deception was over. Oriana would tell Nye, and he would be free from the strangling secret at last.

But the expression on Oriana's face—her lovely features contorted with anger, fury—cut him to the core. That bothered him far more than Nye's reaction now. He didn't love Nye like he loved Oriana.

Loved.

Nicanor straightened and took a step backward on the shoveled walkway, his balance suddenly unsteady. He had tried not to let it happen, but it had. Somewhere between her smiles and tears, he began to love her.

And she ordered him out with the same hatred he had

heard in his father's voice a thousand times. He could not imagine a worse punishment.

The bush at the end of the path rustled. A boy shot out from between the last two plants and darted to the sidewalk.

Dez.

Nicanor ran after him almost before he realized who the boy was. He chased him down the sidewalk, through a yard, past another apartment building—dodging icy patches on the ground as he ran.

The boy sprinted across a street in front of a car that cut Nicanor off.

Nicanor waited for the yelling driver to move the car, then took off again, pushing himself faster.

The boy could really run.

Nicanor closed in as they neared the bus stop. He reached out and snagged Dez by the back of his jacket collar.

He squirmed and kicked, trying to strike Nicanor's legs.

Nicanor jerked the boy by the jacket and dragged him to the bench at the bus stop. He slammed Dez onto the bench and pinned down his arms as he fought to escape.

"What were you doing at Oriana's apartment?" Nicanor barked in the boy's face.

"None of your business." He tried to get up, but Nicanor held him down.

"Maybe I won't call the police. Maybe I'll deal with you myself." Nicanor leaned over so that his face was just inches from the boy's obnoxious glare. "You worthless punk—I should show you what it's like—what you did to her."

The defiance dropped away and fear flashed in his eyes. "I just wanted to see her."

"Why?" Nicanor yelled. "So you could laugh at what you did?"

"I wanted to tell her I'm sorry." He lowered his gaze as he turned to jelly under Nicanor's hands, the fight gone from his body. "I'm sorry," he whispered. He glanced up, then away again.

The brief glimpse at the boy's eyes was enough. Nicanor was staring in a mirror—the unbearable guilt, the utter despair. He straightened, releasing the fugitive.

Dez pulled up his knees and wrapped his arms around his legs to hold them to his chest.

You worthless rat! The words of Nicanor's father echoed in his mind, as he looked at the image of himself in his protective pose. *You should die for what you did,* the old man yelled, disgust and hatred twisting his features.

Right again, Papá.

"Go," Nicanor said to the boy.

"What?" Dez looked up at him, startled.

"Get out of here before I turn you in. Do not let me catch you here again."

Dez slowly stood up from the bench. "Would you tell her? Tell her I'm sorry?"

"No. She will never forgive you." She could never forgive either of them. "Being sorry isn't enough. You will have to live with what you did. So will she. Sorry doesn't fix it." And that was Nicanor's ultimate stupidity—believing that somehow staying alive, helping Nye, loving Oriana, would change anything. That it could somehow undo the horror and devastation of what he had done to everyone he cared about.

He looked at Dez, coming out of his thoughts just enough to notice the anguish on the boy's face. Nicanor knew from experience, it would only get worse.

Dez silently turned and walked away, his small shoulders slumped under his oversized jacket.

Nicanor watched him go, wondering what the boy was planning if he wasn't going to take the bus back downtown. Nicanor made himself look away and sat on the bench to wait for the bus. His help wasn't wanted, his concern worthless—Oriana had made that clear. Her eyes and her words said the same thing as his father—she wished he was dead.

It was over. There was nothing left to try, nothing left to do. If he couldn't make things better, if he could not be forgiven, then he had only one option. He had to pay the only way he knew how.

The brakes of the bus squealed and whooshed as it stopped in front of him. He got on automatically. He saw no one and heard nothing as the bus took him back to the squalor he belonged in.

This Shadow

He didn't know how long he walked up and down the streets after he got off the bus. Nighttime was better. No chance of being interrupted or discovered until it was done. So he kept moving, trying not to think as he wandered, waiting for the shadow in his soul to cover the sky.

At last, the sun sank on the horizon and the world went dark.

Nicanor walked the now familiar route to the store and silently bought one whiskey bottle from the drunk owner.

The night air as Nicanor went to the apartment building was cold, the staircase stank as usual, his apartment still in decay, but none of it mattered. He only saw Dante's hand, reaching desperately out of the water. He smelled his father's whiskey-laden breath. He heard Oriana's scream from her hospital bed.

He picked up the bottle of sleeping pills from the floor, next to the mattress. He only had the two doses left, but the whiskey would make it work.

What was that verse he read? Something about the penalty for sin being death.

Nicanor dumped the pills into his mouth and swallowed them, cringing at the bitter taste as they went down. He opened the whiskey bottle, took a deep breath, and drank every drop.

He let the bottle go. It smashed on the floor. He went to his mattress, laid down on his back, and prepared to pay the penalty for his lifetime of wrongs. The image of Oriana's eyes, full of hatred, filled his vision. He would miss her smile.

Chapter Seventeen

*"Then they cried to the Lord in their trouble,
and he delivered them from their distress.
He brought them out of darkness
and the shadow of death,
and burst their bonds apart."*
– Psalm 107:13-14

Oriana's watch chimed the hour. If her count was right, the time was eight p.m. She didn't know how long it had been since her tears finally dried up. She still sat on the floor, now leaning her back against the side of the armchair. She had no reason to move, no reason to stand up, no reason to do anything.

She thought she had learned her lesson on naiveté, but it hadn't been thorough enough. For here she was, shattered once again because she had trusted someone. Because she had looked through the blind eyes of love. She didn't know she loved him until he told her the truth, and she felt a kind of pain she had never known. It tore at her insides, racking her body with uncontrollable sobs. This horror must be a broken heart.

A dead soul and a broken heart. What was left for this darkness to devour?

The stair outside the apartment creaked. Footsteps.

Oriana got to her feet. Was it Nicanor? She held her breath, both wanting and not wanting it to be him.

There was a sound she didn't recognize, like a gentle thump on the wall by her door. Then the footsteps took off, fast and lighter than she had heard before.

Like a child's.

Dez. They could get to her apartment now. They could get inside if they wanted.

She waited, not making a sound until she was sure he was gone. This time.

Would he be back with James? What was the noise he had made outside her door?

Fearing what sort of booby trap she might find, Oriana reached the door and slowly opened it.

Nothing happened.

Careful not to step out, she crouched and patted her hand along the floor next to the door. She touched something hard. It didn't feel very big as she moved her fingers over it. The object was smooth, like polished wood. She stopped. It was a cross.

The memory of Dez's words, from so long ago, sprang to her mind. "James says people like you talk about Jesus 'cause you never had anything bad happen to you."

Her stomach lurched. He was mocking her.

She stood, bracing herself with one hand on the doorframe while she clutched the cross in the other.

If they were going to kill her so she couldn't testify, why didn't they just do it? Why the sadistic game?

Maybe she could end it. A strange sense of hope came with the realization. She wouldn't have to live with this pain. She wouldn't have to see the darkness of tomorrow. All she had to do was give herself up and let them kill her.

She jammed her feet into the boots she had left by the door and stumbled out, catching herself on the railing along the wall. She counted the steps as she went down them quickly, trying not to fall. She reached the bottom and managed to find her way to the front door.

She felt for the knob and pushed the door open.

A bitter wind slapped her face as she stepped out, forgetting about the small drop to the path. She gripped the doorknob tightly to keep from falling.

Was that a noise in the bushes?

"I know you're there, Dez."

No response.

She let go of the door, walking out on the path as it swung shut behind her. "James?" She hoped they couldn't hear the quiver in her voice. If they were there.

She slowed, listening. Was it just the wind rustling the bushes? Or were they there, watching her, laughing at her?

She heard something. She followed the noise. The wind blew from a new direction. Had she gone beyond the bushes to the sidewalk? She tried to remember what it all looked like, how far the distances were and how far she had just gone. She turned back and reached for the bushes. Her fingers grabbed only air.

She had gone too far. Her stomach twisted. She didn't know where she was. "Dez, if you're there, just get it over with. Or James, I don't care."

The silence terrified her more than an answer.

"Dez!" she yelled.

She was afraid to move. What if she stepped into the street or crashed into something? But she couldn't just stand there. She would freeze. She hadn't even thought to put on a jacket.

Panic surged up her throat as she took a few steps, desperately hoping to get her bearings somehow. Was the apartment building in front of her? Or behind her?

The wind bit at her cheeks, and her fingers started to ache from the cold. She had to get inside.

She started to walk, sticking her hands out in front of her and bracing to crash into something at any moment. The ground suddenly went higher, and she tripped, falling on her hands into something fairly soft ... and wet. Snow. She pushed herself up, wincing from the impression the cross had made on her fingers when she fell, the pain exaggerated because her hands were freezing from the snow that soaked them.

She trudged on, lifting her feet higher in the deep snow. Wet clumps fell into her boots, shocking her ankles with cold. The snow became even deeper. Her legs, weak from sitting around the apartment, quickly tired. She tried to take another step, but her foot stuck in the snow. She fell on her hands and knees, losing the cross.

Snow sprayed her face, mixing with tears she thought she had used up. Her heart ached like it was being squeezed in a vise. "What do You want from me?" she cried out to God. She threw her head back to look straight up, but there was only darkness there. "Where is Your love now?" She lifted her numb hands, wet snow falling off them. "Why?" she screamed.

Sobs shook her body as she leaned her head in her hands, slowly collapsing until she lay on the snow-covered ground, weeping. She had no more strength. She was finished.

Is this how she would die? Separated from the God she had spent her life trying to serve? In utter despair and failure, defeated by the darkness?

She slid her hand out along the snow as she wept. Her fingers, almost completely numb, bumped something hard. She stretched out her hand to feel it.

The cross.

As she rested her fingers on the wet wood, the rest of the passage that she had quoted to Nicanor, a part she once knew by heart, came to her mind as clearly as if someone was speaking the words to her. "Who shall separate us from the love of Christ?" she whispered, through the taste of tears and snow. "Shall trouble or hardship or persecution or famine or nakedness or danger or sword? As it is written: 'For your sake we face death all day long; we are considered as sheep to be slaughtered.' No ..." she gripped the cross and planted her other hand in the snow to slowly push herself up as her voice grew louder, "... in all these things we are more than conquerors through Him who loved us."

The truth she thought she had known dawned in her soul with a searing light that warmed her from within. Why couldn't she see it before? Beyond the shattered walls of her fairytale world, there was indeed a great darkness. But in that darkness there stood a cross where Jesus Christ, the Lord of the universe, suffered and died ... for her. Only when she stood in the shadow of that cross could she see the light of the glorious heaven behind it.

"In all things God works for the good of those who love him," she quoted, remembering how much those words had stung in her wounds only hours earlier. "Oh, Lord. When did I stop believing Your promise? When did I stop believing in You? Father, forgive me."

Then God can't forgive everything. Nicanor's anguished plea echoed in her memory.

She closed her eyes. "Dear God. What have I done?" She squeezed the wooden cross until it hurt even through the numbness. "Lord, You paid for my sin on the cross. I know I'm forgiven. If I should die here, please don't let what I did keep Nicanor from coming to You and receiving Your forgiveness." She drew her knees in and hugged them to her chest. "Show him Your light, Father, as You've shown it to me." She rested her head on her knees as a shiver shook her body. "Your good and perfect will be done," she whispered and closed her eyes.

"Miss Sanders?"

She must be imagining things ... or dreaming. Did people get hallucinations before they froze to death?

"Miss Sanders?" The voice was closer. A boy's. Dez?

Oriana opened her eyes and disregarded the continual blackness. She was too busy listening.

"Are you okay, Miss Sanders?" It was him, though his voice was strained, devoid of the macho bravado it had always held before.

She waited for the anger, hate, or even fear, but her heart warmed with love. Dez had come back. He could be there just to hurt her again, but she wasn't scared. Nothing could separate her from God's love, not Dez, not even her weak faith and self-reliant pride.

His jacket rustled as he trudged over to her. He took in a quick shaky gasp, like trying to hold back tears.

Was he crying?

"I didn't know what ... I'm sorry ... I'm so sorry." His words faded into uneven breaths and heaves of desperate weeping.

Her newly repaired heart ached at the young boy's pain. She did what she had never been free to do before. She held out her arms, and he threw himself into her embrace. She didn't think of the cold as she held the sobbing boy there, on the snow. She thought only of God's miraculous grace.

"I forgive you," she whispered in Dez's ear.

He slowly pulled back, his crying dwindling to a few sniffles. "Because Jesus is in your heart?"

He remembered. "Yes, Dez." She smiled. "Because Jesus is in my heart."

"That's why I gave you the cross. Do you like it?"

And she had thought the gifts were to taunt her. She covered a sigh at how blinded she had been by the darkness she had let grow inside her. "I like it very much. It was just what I needed."

"Ain't—aren't you cold without a jacket?"

She laughed. Just a short, slight laugh, but the first since her blindness. It felt like the taste of air after nearly suffocating. "Yes, I am. Could you help me get inside?"

"Sure. Grab my arms."

She did as he instructed, and he helped her up with surprising strength. "Thank you. I'll put my hand on your arm, and you can lead me back home. How far away are we?"

"The bushes and the path are just right over there."

So close to safety and yet hopelessly lost. Hopeless, if not for God.

"Did you like the tree?" Dez thankfully went slowly as they trudged through the snow.

"Oh." She hesitated, then decided on honesty. "I didn't get

a chance to take it out and really feel it yet."

"LaTisha won't like that. You better look at it. Or feel it or whatever. She and the other kids decorated it. She wanted me to tell you that she even let Maria help."

Thank you, Lord. God had used Oriana even when she was doing things wrong. He was using her to reach these kids. There was hope.

"Oriana?"

Oriana turned her head toward the sound of a woman's voice. "Mrs. Peters?"

"Watch out," Dez warned. "The snow stops. You gotta step down to the sidewalk."

Adult hands took Oriana's other arm as she stepped carefully down. "Oh, my dear, you're freezing." Mrs. Peters felt Oriana's forehead with an experienced mother's touch. "What are you doing out here without a coat?"

"It's a long story. I'm just thankful you're both here now."

"I came back early from church. Nye called me and asked that the church pray and that I come and get you." Mrs. Peters delivered the words in rapid-fire without a breath, clearly upset.

"What is it?" Nye touched Mrs. Peters' warm hand, which rested on her arm. "What's wrong?"

"It's your friend, Nicanor. Nye found him at his apartment and the ambulance took him to the hospital."

Oriana's heart stopped. "What … " She couldn't get out any more than that.

"They don't know how he is yet." Mrs. Peters put something warm over Oriana's shoulders, probably the kind woman's coat. "We need to get you warm first, and then I'll take you there." Her tone signaled there would be no convincing her to take Oriana to the hospital straightaway.

There was nothing to do but cooperate, wait … and pray. Pray desperately that God would give her another chance to show His love to Nicanor.

"Nicky … Nicky," his mother whispered.

"Jesus loves me, this I know. For the Bible tells me so …" he sang in a little boy's voice.

His mother's blonde hair blew softly around her face, tendrils lightly caressing her cheeks. She smiled, and her blue eyes sparkled. "I love you, Nicky. And Jesus loves you even more. Never forget …"

"Nicanor. Can you hear me?"

A different woman's voice came to Nicanor in the midst of the vivid dream—or was it a memory?

"Nicanor?"

He slowly opened his eyes.

Nye looked down at him, her loose blonde hair like his dream. She smiled. "You're awake."

Then he had failed. Even from his back, lying on a bed, he knew he was in a hospital room. The pain was supposed to be over. He was not supposed to have to face Nye, to tell her the truth and watch her hate him as much as Oriana did. "How do you feel?"

"I saw her." Nicanor's words came out weak and hoarse.

Nye's brow furrowed. "Who?"

He swallowed. "My mother."

Nye moved back, and he turned his head to see her sit down in a chair next to the bed. "Do you often dream of her?"

"Never. I forgot ..." His voice failed.

"What did you forget?"

He turned his head to look at the ceiling. "Something she taught me."

"Something important?"

"I killed her, you know." Telling her that was easier than telling her the truth about Dante.

"Is that what your father told you?"

A cough forced its way out, scraping his dry throat. "He was right. I got sick, gave it to her."

"And she died. That wasn't your fault. She wouldn't want you to blame yourself for that, would she?"

Nye was always calm now. When had the romantic young dancer he knew turned into such a wise soul?

He swallowed again and waited for the question she really wanted to ask. Perhaps he would have a long wait. She didn't like to be personal. "You want to know why I did it." He had to get this over with.

"If you want to tell me."

He sighed and closed his eyes. He felt so tired, so terribly tired. Forcing himself to open his heavy lids, he tried to focus his thoughts into something coherent. "I have never told you the truth. About Dante and … that day." He stared at the ceiling, the anxiety building in his stomach making him more awake. "I was high when I took the boat out. On cocaine. I saw him fall out of the boat when the wave hit us. I didn't help him. I was too …" He took a ragged breath. "I'm sorry, *pajarita*." He hoped calling her by the nickname he had given her long ago would bring relief, but it only made the burden of memories heavier.

"Oh, Nicanor. I know all of that."

He turned his head to look at her.

A single tear tracked down her cheek. "Dante told me you were high before he went with you. That's why we fought about it. I didn't want him to go, and he said he had to because he was scared for you."

Nicanor stared at her, not believing she could have known all this time. How could she have treated him as kindly as she had? "Then you know that I have to pay for what I did. I gave up drugs, but it wasn't enough. I tried to pay … I failed."

"No, *I* failed." She leaned toward him. "I am so sorry. I told you I was wrong to blame you all those years, but I don't think I ever told you that I forgave you. For everything."

"How … How could you?"

"In the eyes of God, I've made mistakes just as awful as yours, but God sent His son to pay for my sins. And for yours. He says that I'm to forgive others, the way He forgave me. It's only because of what Jesus did for me, dying on the cross so that my wrongs are wiped clean forever, only because of His sacrifice and forgiveness that I can forgive you."

Nicanor moistened his dry lips. "You sound like Dante."

"I'm glad. He was right. He would have wanted to be the one to die, you know."

Nicanor looked at her. How could she say that?

"He was already saved. You weren't." She gave him a small smile.

Saved. Was that what enabled Nye to look at him with the love of a friend? "You should hate me."

"I don't."

"Oriana does."

Nye blinked. "I can't believe that."

"She's right. I have to pay."

"You can't, no matter how hard you try or what you do to yourself. I think you know that better than most people. Jesus loves you, Nicanor. He paid for what you did. You just need to believe that and put your faith in Him. Ask for His forgiveness, and He'll give it to you."

A deep desire stirred inside Nicanor's weary soul as he rested his head back and looked up. Could it be true? Could he really be forgiven and freed from this hell he had been living in? "How do I do that?"

"May I tell him?"

Oriana? Nicanor turned his head, and his heart leapt at the beautiful sight of Oriana, led into the room by none other than Dez. The boy's presence was hard to comprehend, but Nicanor wanted only to focus on Oriana. There was something different about her. As she drew nearer and Nye stood to help her into the chair, he saw what was changed. Her eyes flashed with the sparkle—the vibrant, pulsating energy that used to make him look away.

"Nicanor?" There was no hatred, no anger on her face, as she rested her hands on the edge of the bed.

"I'm here."

"I'm sorry. I said horrible things to you that I never should have. If I had lost you because of that, or if I pushed you away from God …" She took in a shaky breath. "I don't know how I'd ever forgive myself."

Warmth coursed through Nicanor's veins as he realized what she was saying. It sounded as if she forgave him. Almost as if she cared for him. He reached over and covered her hand with his. "No apologies."

"Does that mean you forgive me?"

"If you forgive me."

"Weren't you going to tell him how to get *God's*

forgiveness?" Nye's eyes glistened with tears as she gently teased her sister.

"Yeah." Oriana's lips turned up into a shy, heart-stealing smile.

Nicanor was sure the machine he was hooked up to would give away his surging pulse when she turned her hand up and clasped his.

"Me, too?" Dez came up to stand next to Oriana.

She reached her other hand out for Dez to grasp. "Absolutely."

When she closed her eyes and began to pray, the shadow that had shrouded Nicanor's life for as long as he could remember began to lift, and he saw what hope looked like—a drug dealer and a murderer holding the hands of a saint, as she led them toward the light.

Epilogue

"You will forget your misery;
you will remember it as waters that have passed away.
And your life will be brighter than the noonday;
its darkness will be like the morning.
And you will feel secure, because there is hope ..."
– Job 11:16-18

Oriana smiled at the joyous sounds that floated to where she sat in the corner of the living room. Christmas was still the most incredible time of the year, even if she couldn't see. Besides, she had experienced enough of her parents' famous Christmas Eve parties through the years to be able to picture it all in her mind. Nye was at the piano, Cullen's baritone joining with her soprano as the only two on-key voices in the mix of jolly visitors who sang familiar carols.

Oriana's mom had gone to the kitchen to freshen the punch and bring out more hors d'oeuvres and desserts than they could possibly eat. Her dad was doing his usual deft job of mingling with adults and performing damage control with the few kids that were running around.

The sound of the children's laughter brought the image of

Dez to Oriana's mind, and her smile faltered.

"Trying to hide or soaking it all in?" Gabe Kelly's deep rumble dropped from his great height.

Oriana grinned. "I didn't think your singing was *that* bad."

He sat in the armchair near hers. "You must not have been listening." He laughed—a hearty and contagious sound.

"I was just thinking about Dez." She didn't want to ruin the levity of the party, but she felt a need to share with the officer who was so involved.

"Have you heard from him?"

"He called me once. I guess they have a nicer apartment there, and his mom got a job right away."

"Good. The change of city might save him. Hopefully keep him from ending up like his brother."

Oriana swallowed. "I can't help thinking that it might be my fault James was killed. Maybe because he was trying to hide from—"

"No, ma'am. He chose that path himself. He was bound to get shot or OD sooner or later the way he was headed. So he got shot. You're not to blame."

"You really can call me Oriana now, you know." She smiled. "'Ma'am' is nice, but it makes me feel old."

He chuckled. "It's the Southern boy in me."

"Well, I'm thankful for that. You were so helpful with all this. I appreciate your kindness."

"Just part of the job, ma'am … Oriana."

"Thanks all the same, Gabe."

He cleared his throat. "You're welcome."

She heard him stand.

"I see a certain someone waiting to talk to you, if I'm not mistaken, and I don't think he wants me around." There was a jovial dose of humor in Gabe's voice. "I'll make myself scarce."

Oriana grinned. "Thanks." Her heart fluttered as she waited for that certain someone she hoped was Nic.

"It's hard to get you alone."

Warmth coursed through her veins at the sound of his smooth voice in front of her. "Do you have to wait until I'm alone?"

He paused. "Perhaps I don't like to share."

She didn't know triple cartwheels were possible until her heart just did them. Was Nic really flirting with her?

"Come with me."

"Where?"

"You always ask questions. Just come."

He was actually teasing her. An emerging lighter side seemed to be one of the slow, growing changes in him that were happening since he came to faith. She was liking the new Nic. If she had been falling in love before, she was plummeting now.

She put out her hand, and he gently clasped it in his. Her breathing quickened as she let him lead her out of the living room and toward what she thought must be the front door. What was he up to?

She started to get an inkling when he had her wait while he got her coat and handed her boots to put on. This could be good or bad. She had barely seen him since his release from the hospital, and she wondered what his absence meant. Now that he no longer needed to feel obligated to Nye, he had no reason to stay here. He could be trying to distance himself from her before finally leaving for good. Maybe he was taking her outside now so she wouldn't make a public scene when he broke the news to her.

Why had she let herself think that if he became a Christian, he would automatically want a relationship with her? She bit her lip as he helped her into the coat, and she grasped his arm to go outside.

Soft, wet snowflakes touched her cheeks as already fallen snow crunched beneath their feet. The night was cold and still, the air crisp and peaceful.

Nic suddenly stopped and turned to face her. He stood close. "I need to tell you something."

He was going to leave. She could tell from the tension in his voice. She couldn't let him leave without at least trying to give him a reason to stay. "Before you say anything," she rushed to interrupt, "there's something I've been wanting to tell you. I realized through all this stuff that's happened that I've been doing things wrong. With the kids, I mean. I was trying to save them myself, but I can't do that, only God can."

"Oriana—"

"Just hear me out. Please?" She felt a nervous drive to finish before he spoke, as if stopping now would let him leave. "The only thing that got through to Dez and LaTisha, the only thing that changed any of my students in any real way, was the little bit I was able to tell them about Jesus. I thought I could make a difference by showing the kids a better way to live, but that's not good enough."

"Oriana—"

"I need to give them a reason for living the best way. A reason for living at all. I can't do that at Lincoln. So I'm going to start a Christian community center. A place where the kids can come after school, and I'll be free to teach them everything I did before plus what they most need to learn about—the love of Jesus."

"*Cariño.*"

She had no idea what that meant, but the tender way he said the word made her stop.

"Cariño." He gently touched her cheek.

"What do you think?" she whispered, scarcely able to breathe.

"You'll need help." He slid his thumb lightly over her cheek as he cradled her face in his hand.

"Oh, yes. I won't try to do it all myself. I've learned that lesson." She let out a nervous laugh.

"Then you'll let me help?"

Her mouth dropped open. She hadn't even gotten to that part of her pitch yet. "You mean," she sputtered, when she could finally speak, "you aren't going back to New York? To tango?"

"No."

"But won't you miss it? Don't you love tango?"

"My father wanted me to dance, so I did. Later, tango was all I knew."

"So you're not moving back to Argentina either?" She bit her lip.

"I just returned from there. For the last time."

"You—"

"Hush, cariño." He touched her lips with his finger. "My turn. I asked Nye not to tell you. I had to go alone and make peace with my father, to bury him with forgiveness."

"Bury him? Oh, Nic, I'm so sorry."

"*Mi* cariño. So much love for everyone." He touched her other cheek, cradling her head between his hands. "Is there love for me?"

Her breath caught. She couldn't speak.

He laughed, softly, the most glorious sound she thought she had ever heard. "Is this Oriana, without a word? Then I'll speak. I'll say that I love you as I have never loved anyone before. I love you more than myself. I love you more than life, more than all but the Savior you showed me."

How could she speak after that? She thought she had died and gone to heaven. She was surprised she could hear above the pounding of her heart.

He abruptly removed his hands, making Oriana panic for the moment before he spoke again.

"Put out your hand."

Feeling like she was in an exhilarating dream that couldn't possibly be real, she did as he said.

He plunked a wet glob into her hand that she knew at once was snow.

A smile stretched across her face as she felt the soft pile, the perfect flakes of wonder as they melted into her hand. But there was something still there, something solid that didn't melt. She reached with her other hand to feel what it was. A small object—smooth, round, and ... a ring.

"I promise you all of my love for the rest of my life."

Tears sprang to Oriana's eyes at the thick emotion in his voice.

"Will you have a sinner like me?"

Oriana finally found her voice. "If you will have one like me. I love you."

He caught a tear with his thumb as it fell down her cheek. "Ah, mi cariño. No tears. Only joy."

"This is the way I do joy." She sniffed. "Nic? Are you smiling?"

"Yes. And so are you."

Her smile widened. "What does cariño mean?"

"It means this." He gently took her in his arms and kissed her.

Savoring the perfection of the moment, she had no idea what their future might hold. There might be shadows and there might be darkness, but she and Nic would be more than conquerors. God had given them light.

About the Author

Jerusha Agen is a lifelong lover of story--a passion that has led her to a B.A. in English and a highly varied career. In addition to authoring the *Sisters Redeemed Series*, Jerusha co-authored the novellas *A Ruby Christmas* and *A Dozen Apologies* (releasing with Write Integrity Press, February 2014).

Jerusha is also a screenwriter, and several of her original scripts have been produced as films. In addition, Jerusha is a film critic, with reviews featured at the website, www.RedeemerReviews.com.

Visit Jerusha on the Web:
www.SDGwords.com
Twitter: @SDGwords
Facebook: Jerusha Agen – SDG Words

Other Books by Jerusha Agen

This Dance
Book One in the
Sisters Redeemed Series
Available now on Amazon, Kindle, Barnes & Noble, and by special order from most local booksellers.

No love, no pain. No God, no games.

A tragedy three years ago destroyed Nye's rise to the top of the dancing world as an upcoming tango star, and in the process destroyed her reason for living, too. She survived the pain and built a new life resembling nothing like the one she left behind, determined never to hurt again.

Nye's emotional walls hold up perfectly until she meets a handsome lawyer and an elderly landowner. They seem harmless, but one awakens feelings she doesn't want and the other makes her face the God she can't forgive. Will these two men help Nye dance again?

A Ruby Christmas
Coming December 2013

Ruby Joy Buckner, cowgirl, has never left the Lone Star State, but at her father's request, she takes her faithful canine companion and travels the world in search of Nativity pieces. As Ruby collects the pieces, she also collects a few unexpected surprises, including an awareness of the beauty in other cultures, and quite a menagerie of new friends, thanks in part to Yippee Ti Yi Yo who charms everyone they meet.

Ruby's budding awareness of life outside Texas opens her eyes to a world of whimsy, and the Nativity pieces she collects are unusual. Will her father approve her eclectic collection … and the changes that travel brought to Ruby's world?

A Dozen Apologies
Coming February 2014

Mara Adkins, a promising fashion designer, has fallen off the ladder of success, and she can't seem to get up. In college, Mara and her sorority sisters played an ugly game, and Mara was usually the winner. She'd date men she considered geeks, win their confidence, and then she'd dump them publicly.

When Mara begins work for a prestigious clothing designer in New York, she gets her comeuppance. Her boyfriend steals her designs and wins a coveted position. He fires her, and she returns in shame to her home in Spartanburg, South Carolina, where life for others has changed for the better.

Mara's parents, always seemingly one step from a divorce, have rediscovered their love for each other, but more importantly they have placed Christ in the center of that love. The changes Mara sees in their lives cause her to seek Christ. Mara's heart is pierced by her actions toward the twelve men she'd wronged in college, and she sets out to apologize to each of them. A girl with that many amends to make, though, needs money for travel, and Mara finds more ways to lose a job that she ever thought possible.

Mara stumbles, bumbles, and humbles her way toward employment and toward possible reconciliation with the twelve men she humiliated to find that God truly does look upon the heart, and that He has chosen the heart of one of the men for her to have and to hold.

This Redeemer
Book Three in the
Sisters Redeemed Series

Coming 2014!

Look for other books

published by

Write Integrity Press

www.WriteIntegrity.com

and

Pix-N-Pens

Pix-N-Pens Publishing

www.PixNPens.com

Made in the USA
San Bernardino, CA
03 January 2014

Copyright © 2020 by Carla Thorne

All rights reserved.

No part of this book may be reproduced in any form or by any electronic or mechanical means, including information storage and retrieval systems, without written permission from the author, except for the use of brief quotations in a book review.

Cover Design - Najla Qamber Designs

❦ Created with Vellum